T0328732

MOURNING THE CHOSEN ONE . . .

Leslie leaned over and draped her arms around Ariel and Caleb. "I know this is gonna sound crazy . . . but in a way, it's like the best thing that could have happened. Sarah took her fate into her own hands. *Everybody's* fate. She knew the Demon was already beat because we found the cure for the plague. Maybe the only way the Demon could possibly win was if *all* the prophecies were fulfilled. So Sarah made sure that none of the prophecies in the last two lunar cycles could ever come true."

Caleb shook his head. "Why . . ."

Ariel wanted to say something—*anything*—but it was impossible. Her mouth couldn't form the words. She was too confused, too distraught. Leslie must be right. It was the only way any of this could possibly make sense.

"I'm gonna keep Sarah's memory alive," Leslie pledged. "I'm gonna make sure that every single kid on this planet knows what she did for them. She has to live on in people's minds. Forever. Nobody can ever forget her."

Ariel buried her face in Leslie's shoulder and wept softly. "They won't," she whispered.

COUNT DOWN

NOVEMBER

by
Daniel Parker

Simon & Schuster

First Aladdin Paperbacks edition October 1999

Produced by 17th Street Productions,
a division of Daniel Weiss Associates, Inc.
33 West 17th Street, New York, NY 10011

Cover design by Mike Rivilis

Aladdin Paperbacks
An imprint of Simon & Schuster
Children's Publishing Division
1230 Avenue of the Americas
New York, NY 10020

The text of this book was set in 10.5 point Rotis Serif.
Printed and bound in the United States of America
10 9 8 7 6 5 4 3 2 1

ISBN: 978-1-4814-2596-4

Library of Congress Catalog Card Number: 99-65498

To the Schtoons of Choate '88

NOVEMBER

The Ancient Scroll of the Scribes:

In the eleventh lunar cycle,
In the year 5760,
The Demon betrays the False Prophet.
Spurred by the lies and deception
of the Demon's servants,
The False Prophet marches
toward his own doom,
Leading the blinded
Visionaries to death with him.
The Demon drinks blood and eats flesh,
Separating from the Chosen One,
Gathering strength within her camp,
Preparing for the final day when
the two Blessed Visionaries arrive
and the battle will be fought.

Tough care mends flaws.
Try to kill nondefensive spells.
Slips affect sins.
Eleven twenty-three ninety-nine.
Meteors ruin an empty forest.
An animal noisily seeks relief.
Foxes appeal unto wedded demons.
Eleven twenty-five ninety-nine.

The countdown has started . . .

The long sleep is over.

For three thousand years I have patiently watched and waited. The Prophecies foretold the day when the sun would reach out and touch the earth—when my slumber would end, when my ancient weapon would breathe, when my dormant glory would blaze once more upon the planet and its people.

That day has arrived.

But there can be no triumph without a battle. Every civilization tells the same story. Good requires evil; redemption requires sin. The legends are as varied as are the civilizations that spawned them— yet each contains that same nugget of truth.

So I am not alone. The Chosen One awaits me. The flare opened the inner eyes of the Visionaries, those who can join the Chosen One to prevent my reign. But in order for them to defeat me, they must first make sense of their visions.

For you see, every vision is a piece of a puzzle, a puzzle that will eventually form a picture . . . a picture that I will shatter into a billion pieces and reshape in the image of my choosing.

I am prepared. My servants knew of this day. They made the necessary preparations to confuse the Visionaries—all in anticipation of that glorious time when the countdown ends and my ancient weapon ushers in the New Era.

My servants unleashed the plague that reduced the earth's population to a scattered horde of frightened adolescents. None of these children know how or why their elders and youngers perished.

And that was only the beginning.

My servants have descended upon the chaos. They will subvert the Prophecies in order to convert the masses into unknowing slaves. They will hunt down the Visionaries, one by one, until all are dead. They will eliminate the descendants of the Scribes so that none of the Visionaries will learn of the scroll. The hidden codes shall remain hidden. Terrible calamities and natural disasters will wreak havoc upon the earth. Even the Chosen One will be helpless against me.

I *will* triumph.

November

PART I

November 1–10, 1999

CHAPTER ONE

Mount Rainier National Park
Washington
November 1–4

The time had finally come.

Even now, Dr. Harold Wurf couldn't quite believe that he was about to meet his destiny. He was about to be *transformed*. From man to immortal. From flesh and blood to divinity. The dark mountain loomed ahead of him—illuminated against the black sky with the glow of a hundred campfires. The distant spots of light were like fireflies . . . continually vanishing and reappearing, blinking in and out of the swaying canopy of trees. The autumn wind howled. His long brown hair flapped over his face and shoulders. The vision was surreal, *awesome*. Thousands of believers were waiting for him there. Tens of thousands.

"This is the place," Linda Altman whispered beside him.

Harold nodded. "I know."

"It's just how I saw it," she said. "I saw the lights and the—"

"I *know*," Harold grumbled, rolling his eyes. "You told me already." He strode across the empty parking lot toward the trail entrances hidden in the shadows of the forest. When would this girl ever learn to keep quiet? Hard to believe that only a few short months ago he would have been content to listen to her babble on and on for hours. Of course, that was when he fooled himself into thinking that her whiny English accent sounded like music. That was when he could stand to look at her for more than a few seconds at a time. . . .

It was such a waste, really. He shook his head. Linda's hideously maimed face would never fully heal. She would never be beautiful again. Years of medical training left no doubt in Harold's mind about that.

Still, the Demon's mysterious attack on that remote highway served a purpose. Yes. It enabled him to see her for who she really was. He'd been blinded by her dazzling looks: the cheekbones, the blue eyes, the blond hair, all of it. He never realized that she was a sycophantic pest—like all the rest of his followers. A little more intelligent, a little more powerful, to be sure . . . but in the end, just another slave.

"Where are you going?" she called.

"To greet my flock," he answered without turning around. *Idiot,* he added silently. Maybe she wasn't so bright. Where did she *think* he was going?

"No, no!" she cried. She ran to catch up with him and clamped her hand down on his shoulder. "You have to wait for the sign—"

"Let go of me," he snapped. He wrenched free of her and whirled around. His nose immediately wrinkled. Even in the darkness the slashes and scars across her face stood out in stark relief against her skin. He lowered his eyes. If he had to spend one

6

more hour alone with her, he didn't think he'd be able to keep himself from running away.

"I—I'm sorry," she stammered. "I didn't mean to touch you. But it's not time."

He gritted his teeth, struggling to maintain an appearance of civility. "What do you mean? We're *here*. It doesn't make sense, Linda. We've been traveling in circles for weeks. I've done everything you said to avoid the Demon. I haven't seen another living soul besides *you* in over a month." He jerked a hand at the mountain. "Now my flock is waiting for me—"

"But the Demon is still close by," she protested. "Look at the sky, Harold. That cloud is the Demon's work. But soon it will melt away. The sun will shine again. And the Demon will grow weak. That's the sign we have to wait for. Until then—"

"How do you *know* all this?" he snapped, glaring at her.

Her lips quivered. "I—I saw it."

"You saw it," he echoed flatly. "You know, it's funny. You see a lot of things, Linda. And not all of them come true."

For the briefest instant a change seemed to come over Linda's expression. Her eyes narrowed very slightly, almost imperceptibly. Was she angry? He peered at her and blinked—but her face was once again frightened and servile. Had he imagined it? She had no right to be upset. None at all . . .

"When have I ever had a vision that didn't come true?" she asked.

He sneered. "A couple of months ago, when we were wandering around the desert. Remember? You

7

told me that a girl was going to appear from the east, bearing an ancient scroll that would be the final key to defeating the Demon. Those were *your* words, Linda. Whatever happened to this girl? Did she have something better to do?"

Linda shook her head. "I . . . I—"

"So what am I supposed to believe?" he demanded, silencing her. His voice rose. His face grew hot. "What if you're wrong about this, too? What if I wait too long? Let me tell you something, Linda. I know a little bit about human nature. If any of the kids on this mountain see me hanging around here, doing nothing, *waiting* for something to happen— then they're going to start wondering why. And then they'll start saying to themselves: 'Gee, maybe the Chosen One isn't really all he says he is.' And *then* I'll have a crisis on my hands."

"But how can you say that?" she cried. "What about your miracles? They wouldn't be here if they didn't know about all the things you did—"

"Oh, shut up. Nobody gives a damn about what I did in the past. Teenagers forget things pretty quickly, in case you haven't noticed. It's happened again and again, no matter *what* I do." He smirked in disgust. "Sometimes I think life is unfair. I mean, Moses was given the Israelites. What did I get? The MTV generation. They can't remember what happened five minutes ago, much less five *months* ago."

Linda didn't reply. She stared back at him, her face blank. But then, to his utter shock, she laughed.

"Is something *funny?*" he spat, enraged.

"No," she murmured. She stared down at the dark

pavement. "It's just that *you've* forgotten something. You have the power to heal anyone, at any time." A sad smile spread across her lips. "You're your own greatest doubter, Harold. You only need to lay your hands on a person and all their ills are cured. . . ." Her voice trailed off.

Harold held his breath. She was right, wasn't she?

He'd cured the plague with a mere touch. He'd destroyed hundreds of nonbelievers with sheer *will*. He was the Healer, first and foremost. If he had to wait for this cloud to lift, nobody would dare second-guess him. Not now.

And the fact remained that Linda had only been wrong once. Every other vision came true . . . often with terrifying and deadly repercussions. He'd let his frustrations with her cloud his judgment. He shook his head. He knew better than that. He was a *genius*.

"Can I ask you something?" she whispered, glancing up at him.

He nodded distractedly.

"Why haven't you healed *me?*"

Harold stared at her stupidly. "I—I . . . I didn't—I don't know," he stammered. For once in his life he had no idea what to say. The thought had never even occurred to him. Why not?

Linda sighed and looked into his eyes. "Look, Harold—I can't explain why that girl never appeared with the scroll," she said finally. "I *saw* it. Maybe the Demon stopped her from coming, or maybe the Demon planted that vision in my mind for some reason. But all I know is that . . . is that . . ." Her voice grew strained. "All I know is that you have to be patient, or else something terrible will happen. The power to produce miracles is in your hands. You just have to do it the right way."

Before he was even aware of it, he found himself reaching out and gently patting the top of her head. He still couldn't bring himself to touch that mutilated flesh or even to say any words . . . but his thoughts were pure.

I'm sorry, Linda. If it's possible for me to heal you, I will. I promise.

"Harold! Harold, wake up!"

He groaned and shook his head. He was too tired—

"It's a miracle! A miracle!"

Just a few more minutes. I need to sleep.

"Look at me, Harold!" Linda shrieked.

Scowling, Harold forced open his eyelids. What time was it, anyway? When had they gone to sleep? It was still black as night—as always. Dark branches swayed in the air above him. He was lying in the dirt . . . and squinting up at a face. But it was so blurry. He didn't even recognize it. Maybe he was dreaming. It belonged to some beautiful woman. . . .

"You healed me!" she cried.

Linda?

He gasped and bolted upright. *My God.* He could hardly breathe. Linda's face . . . it was right there, right in front of him—only it was pristine and unblemished, far more gorgeous than he had ever even remembered. He furiously rubbed his eyes, struggling to clear his vision. His gaze roved over every detail:

the subtle curve of her full lips, the tiny button nose, the rosy cheeks. . . . But there wasn't a scar to be found. And her face was *thinner,* somehow. Sexier. Her eyes possessed a sly, seductive sparkle he'd never seen. Yes, yes. He started to smile. She must have lost weight these past few weeks. She certainly hadn't been eating well. But the transformation was unbelievable—

"You did it, Harold," she whispered, throwing her arms around him. "You made it go away. You saved me."

"When did it happen?" he forced himself to ask. His throat was dry, scratchy. His head pounded. He almost felt hungover. Was this *real?*

"Sometime last night," she whispered in his ear. "I woke up, and my entire body was tingling. It was like somebody plugged me into a socket. I was . . . I don't even know how to describe it, Harold. I was *electrified.* And then I ran my hands over my face. No more bumps. No more scabs. No more pain. You *did* it."

Slowly the realization began to sink in. His eyes widened. All he had to do was wish for her to be healed, and she was. It was a totally unselfish act. He wanted her to be stunning again, for *her* sake—not for his. He nodded.

That must be it! The secret behind his power: lack of self-interest.

Of course. Back in the Promised Land, he'd cured Luke—stopped the plague even as the boy was melting. And the same criterion applied. He'd wanted to prevent Luke from dying. That had been his only motive. It was the doctor inside him—in his soul. He'd almost forgotten why he'd wanted to practice medicine in the first place: to *help* people.

"I was wrong, Harold," Linda sobbed. "You shouldn't hide until the time is right. You should go to greet your flock. You should heal as many of them as possible before you get the sign. Every miracle you perform weakens the Demon. I can *feel* it."

Yes, Harold thought. *I can feel it, too.* She'd been right all along. He was his own greatest doubter. But not anymore. Today he would stride forth and take charge of his followers, with this beautiful Visionary at his side. He would prepare them for the coming day—when he would stretch out his hand over the multitude and grant them all the blessing of immortality.

Together they would inherit the earth. And he would rule them for eternity. He didn't know exactly *how* it would happen . . . or even when that day would arrive. The details would manifest themselves at the appropriate time, as they always did. He only knew that he would do the impossible.

Because now he knew the truth.

He wasn't just a god. He was *the* God. Yes. The moment of epiphany was upon him. He leaned back and smiled at her.

"Thank you, Harold," she choked out.

Amazing, he marveled. Even her voice was sweeter.

187 Puget Drive,
Babylon, Washington
November 1

If Sarah isn't here, I doubt I'll ever find her. She could have chased Jezebel halfway across the state by now.

Ariel Collins stood shivering outside her old house. It was cold. Too cold for November. Of course, it might not even *be* November. It might be the end of October. It might be four in the morning or four in the afternoon. There was no way to tell. In the endless night that had fallen over Babylon, it was impossible to keep track of time. She wondered for a moment if that cheap old Mickey Mouse clock was still ticking away upstairs on her bureau. . . .

Well, why don't you go in there and look, dummy?

But she couldn't quite move. Not yet. The place didn't exactly beckon her with a warm, fuzzy feeling. It didn't even look like *hers*. At least, not the way she remembered it. It looked more like a haunted house from some cheap theme park—ghostly and shadowy against the blackness of the sky.

The front door was open. Had she left it that way? She couldn't remember. She leaned forward and squinted across the lawn . . . and saw the slope of the

13

staircase banister in the hall. *Man.* It was amazing how well her eyes had adjusted to the lack of light. Over a week of dusk worked wonders for a person's vision. If the sun ever did come out again, she'd probably go blind.

"Sarah?" she called quietly. "Sarah, are you in there? Can you . . ."

She shut her mouth. Something about whispering in the dark made her feel edgy and uncomfortable . . . as if she were a wacko, jabbering away to an imaginary friend. She probably *was* talking to herself. The street was deserted, just like every other street in Babylon. Everybody was hanging around the stinking vat of medicine at the Washington Institute of Technology—hiding from the Demon (wherever she was), cowering together in the darkness, scarfing down that magical cure for the melting plague and trying not to yack.

Anyway, why would Sarah have come *here?* Sarah was looking for Jezebel. And Jezebel had always made a point of avoiding this place—even *before* the plague hit last December, and long before people knew who she really was. She once had the gall to claim that the only reason she ever "stooped" to go to Ariel's was to get wasted.

Like on New Year's Eve.

Yup. It all began right here. *Casa de* Collins. Ariel shook her head in disgust. She hadn't thought about that lame excuse for a party in a long time—mainly because her father and about six billion other people happened to melt into puddles of black goo that night. But looking back on it now, she was amazed at how easily Jezebel had fooled everyone. The girl was a supreme actress. She'd thrown a fit, pretending to be frightened out of her mind—when all the while *she* was responsible for the blackout, for the plague . . . for all of it.

Well, actually, that might not be true. According to Sarah, the Demon took control of Jezebel's body in April. Before that, Jezebel was still herself—the same insecure bitch Ariel had known most of her life. So maybe Jez *had* been scared that night. And Sarah should know the truth. She knew everything. She was the Chosen One.

"Sarah?" Ariel called again, a little more urgently.

The house didn't answer.

You shouldn't have gone out looking for her, Ariel told herself. *You don't know what's out here. Sarah went to battle the Demon. This is way over your head. You should have waited for her to come back to WIT—like everyone else.*

Yeah. She *should* have waited. But she couldn't stand the place any longer. For one thing, the stench of the plague antidote was burning a hole in her nose. Besides, how could she just sit there and wonder? Ariel had never been able to do that: to kick back and let life run its course. It was no surprise that so many people used to think she was the Demon. She was always looking for a way to take control of a situation, to be in charge. Always.

She was here. She *had* to take a quick peek inside.

Okay. She shoved her hands into her pockets and shuffled quickly across the dry lawn. Her feet crunched in the grass. Maybe she'd go up to her room and—

Ariel paused in midstep.

There was something on the floor, just inside the doorway.

Oh, my . . .

Her legs instantly gave out from under her.

Sarah.

Her entire midsection was soaked in blood. And she wasn't alone. Jezebel lay nearby, sprawled on her back at the bottom of the stairs. A foul-smelling odor hung in the air. Huge brown splotches stained the floor. *No, no.* Ariel grasped at the door frame for support, her stomach wrapping itself into a knot. She sank to her knees. *No!* This was all wrong. Both girls were staring up at the ceiling. They were bone white. Unblinking. Unmoving. Wearing that same look of glazed surprise that Trevor had worn when Ariel had found *his* body. . . .

"Sarah?" Ariel croaked.

This was impossible. Sarah must be in shock. She *couldn't* die. What about the necklace? Wasn't it supposed to make her invincible? That's what it had done for Ariel . . . but the chain hung loose around Sarah's neck. The ugly ticktacktoe-shaped silver pendant lay by the side of her head.

Ariel forced herself to crawl across the dark threshold. Her arms trembled convulsively. She grabbed Sarah's shoulders and shook them. But there was no response. Sarah's neck flopped in Ariel's hands like some kind of rubbery plant stalk. Her glasses slipped from her face and clattered to the floor beside the pendant. A gun was clenched in her fingers.

"Sarah!" Ariel shouted. She dug her nails into

Sarah's hard, cold flesh. "Sarah, *please!* Wake up. Wake up!"

Nothing.

This can't be what Sarah's scroll meant. It can't . . .

But the words of the prophecy appeared in her mind, as clearly as if she were reading them from Sarah's notebook: *"Both the Chosen One and the Demon are weakened. . . . They fight bitterly, but neither is victorious."*

Ariel's eyes clouded with tears. Her rocking grew more violent. Sarah had predicted this, hadn't she? That was why she had run off without even saying good-bye. That was why she'd entrusted Ariel with her notebook, with the translation of that magical, three-thousand-year-old Hebrew scroll. She *knew* she was going to die . . . even with the necklace. Jezebel might have stolen the scroll itself, but she couldn't keep the prophecies from coming true.

"Why?" Ariel shrieked, collapsing against Sarah's body. "Why did you have to chase her? Why didn't you stay with me? Why?"

She lay still for a moment—every muscle tensed, every sense poised to detect the slightest murmur or movement.

But Sarah was as lifeless as the floor beneath them.

So that was it. Sarah was dead. Ariel had lost everything. *Everything.*

The awful realization swept over her like a toxic flood. She couldn't deny it. She'd even lost her worst enemy. Jezebel was gone, too—or Lilith, or whoever she really was. There was nobody left. *It's over. My life is over.* Everybody had died—or disappeared like her best friend, Leslie, like her boyfriend, Caleb . . . and like all the others she had known before or after the plague. She was all alone. Forever. All she had left was Sarah's notebook—and the unsolved mysteries inside it.

"Don't do this to me, Sarah," she pleaded. "Please, don't do this."

Her eyes wandered back to the necklace on the floor. Leslie had warned Sarah that it might not be able to protect her. Leslie had warned that Jezebel might be able to twist its magic to *destroy* Sarah. And it looked as if Leslie was right. Or maybe the necklace never had any powers in the first place. Maybe Jezebel had planted it among them to confuse them all.

It didn't matter, though. Whatever the reason, the necklace would never be able to have any more power over *anyone*. No. Jezebel—the Demon—was gone. Ariel gently removed it from Sarah's neck and shoved it into her jeans pocket. *I'm gonna hold on to this,* she swore silently. *Nobody's ever gonna see this thing again. For all I know, it killed you, Sarah. So I'm gonna make sure—*

"Ariel?"

Her head jerked up.

Two silhouettes stood in the doorway. A boy and a girl.

Her eyes narrowed.

Caleb and Leslie? Was she hallucinating? She'd just been thinking about them. . . .

They can't be real. I haven't seen either of them in weeks.

They were like images from a dream . . . a hysterical reaction to the stress and horror. Caleb was wearing a pair of old baggy jeans—with his long bangs in his beautiful, droopy face. And Leslie was as dark and gorgeous as a movie star, her black curls rippling hypnotically in the breeze.

A tremendous, heavy sorrow consumed Ariel. She'd gotten into so many stupid fights with her best friend—mostly because Leslie had been jealous of Ariel's friendship with Sarah. But now those fights seemed far away and meaningless, as if they had happened to two other people in some other lifetime. The only thing that mattered was that Leslie was here.

"What happened?" Leslie gasped.

Ariel just shook her head.

"Are you hurt, Ariel?" Caleb murmured. He crouched beside her. His frightened eyes swept over her body. "Were you shot?"

Shot. The question didn't seem to make any sense. She could only gape at Caleb as he took her in his arms, pulling her away from Sarah's body. His hands were warm; she could feel his breath on her ear.

"What are you doing here?" she finally managed.

"We came to look for you," he whispered. He squeezed her tightly, running a hand through her dirty, brownish blond hair. "We wanted to apologize for everything and . . . God, Ariel. What—" He didn't finish.

"I knew it," Leslie hissed. She was trembling. "I *knew* something bad was going to happen. Didn't I tell you, Caleb? I saw Jezebel running away from Old

Pine Mall. She had a gun." Her words grew strained. "She came here to do something crazy—"

"Just tell us about it, okay, Ariel?" Caleb interrupted. He leaned back and stared into Ariel's eyes. "Did you see it?"

She shook her head again. "I—I—just found them like this," she stammered. Tears began to flow down her cheeks. "I only got here, like, five minutes ago. I think they must have done this to each other. . . ."

"But I don't get it," Leslie mumbled. Her gaze darted between the two bodies. "How could they die? They aren't even *people!* I mean, aren't they, like . . . supernatural beings or something? Where's the necklace? I thought you said it would *save* her!"

For a brief moment Ariel stared at her friend. She opened her mouth, then closed it. She better not tell Leslie the truth. No. Leslie might want the necklace back. She might want to wear it. And even if the Demon was dead, the necklace could still possess some evil power. . . .

"Well?" Leslie demanded.

"It wasn't here," Ariel finally found herself answering. "I don't know where it is."

She glanced back down at Sarah, shoving the lie from her mind. "I know why they died, though. Sarah told me that the prophecies for this lunar cycle would be fulfilled, no matter what." Her brow grew furrowed. "But—but—"

"But what?" Caleb prodded.

"There's one thing I don't get," Ariel went on. "The prophecies aren't over. There's still two more lunar cycles in the scroll. Two months to go."

Caleb's eyes widened. "Until *what?*"

"I don't know. I don't think Sarah did, either. But more stuff was supposed to happen. Something really bad was gonna go down."

"So what does that mean?" Caleb pressed.

Ariel shrugged. She didn't answer. She *couldn't*. Only the Chosen One could.

"You know what I think it means?" Leslie whispered. There was a hint of desperation in her voice. She jerked a finger at the two bodies. "I think it means that this whole thing is over. I don't think that any of the prophecies can come true anymore because the Chosen One and the Demon are both dead. Whatever was supposed to happen ended here."

I wish that were true, Ariel answered silently.

But that sense of dread was still there, buried far beneath the sadness and anger—the unnameable fear that had seized her in April and never let go. And that evil black cloud still hung in the sky. . . .

"Think about it," Leslie added. "Sarah said that most of the prophecies were about the Demon and the Chosen One. Almost *all* of them. So if these two are dead, they can't fulfill any prophecies, right?"

Wait a second.

That was a pretty good point. Maybe Leslie was right. Ariel had glanced a couple of times at the prophecies for the last two lunar cycles. The Demon and the Chosen One were described as if they were still alive. So maybe Sarah knew that the only way to stop this terrible thing from happening—whatever it was—was to end the Demon's life. And her own. The words in the scroll wouldn't have any meaning if the Chosen One and Demon were gone.

"You see what I'm saying?" Leslie asked in the silence.

"Yeah," Caleb whispered. "I do."

Ariel began nodding. "She came here to stop it all."

"Exactly." Leslie leaned over and draped her arms around both of them. "I know this is gonna sound crazy . . . but in a way, it's like the best thing that could have happened. Sarah took her fate into her own hands. *Everybody's* fate. She knew the Demon was already beat because we found the cure for the plague. Maybe the only way the Demon could possibly win was if *all* the prophecies were fulfilled. So Sarah made sure that none of the prophecies in the last two lunar cycles could ever come true."

Caleb shook his head. "Why . . ."

Ariel wanted to say something—*anything*—but it was impossible. Her mouth couldn't form the words. She was too confused, too distraught. Leslie must be right. It was the only way any of this could possibly make sense.

"I'm gonna keep Sarah's memory alive," Leslie pledged. "I'm gonna make sure that every single kid on this planet knows what she did for them. She has to live on in people's minds. Forever. Nobody can ever forget her."

Ariel buried her face in Leslie's shoulder and wept softly. "They won't," she whispered.

The Eleventh Lunar Cycle

The human chameleon had given her last and finest performance.

Over the many long months Naamah had come to learn that her greatest skill was that of improvisation. It was a shame that she wouldn't need it in the New Era. Harold's volatile behavior had honed it so well.

Once again she'd reacted beautifully to a potential crisis . . . sealing Harold's demise.

The boy was truly a chest of loathsome wonders. His revulsion for her had grown so profound that it had overcome everything else. How quickly he forgot his own fear! It was wonderfully ironic. He spoke disdainfully of short attention span—when he himself could no longer remember the terror he felt only weeks ago . . . when he'd first found Linda Altman on that moonlit highway, bruised and scarred beyond recognition.

Yet her plan had nearly backfired. Her phony

injuries were too gruesome, too convincing—even for a onetime medical student. The job was too good, if such a thing were possible. Her new, false ugliness had almost compelled him to leave her . . . in much the same irrational way her beauty had before.

But now Harold's affection for Linda Altman had been restored.

Naamah was poised for victory. When she drugged Harold and scrubbed her makeup clean, he awoke to the belief that he had healed her and made her beautiful again. Even better, he perceived the "healing" to be his crowning achievement—proof positive that his godlike powers were stronger than ever.

And so Naamah no longer feared overconfidence. There was no need. She could afford to revel in her triumph. For the next three weeks she would guide Harold carefully through the majestic wonder of Mount Rainier National Park—greeting those believers who had not yet caught word of the plague antidote, those who still needed to be healed.

Harold still didn't know of the antidote's existence.

And he never would. The weeks of isolation had bolstered his ignorance. He wouldn't believe the truth, even if he learned of it.

And fortunately, nobody on this mountain could tell him.

No . . . her fellow Lilum had cleared the way. They'd arrived at the mountain early, eliminating all those who might cause a problem, then moving discreetly among those who kept coming—watching for any threats. But there were none. All those who had taken the antidote had been murdered and disposed of, their bodies burned as offerings to Lilith in scattered fires that dotted the mountain.

Strangely, Lilith had not yet responded to the sacrifices. Usually there was some sign of appreciation, some subtle hint that Lilith was pleased with her servants' work. But Naamah understood that there might be a very good reason for the lack of communication—a reason she could never know. Lilith was still very far away. She was busy with her own tasks. Tasks that would be finished soon. Very soon . . .

Mount Rainier National Park
Washington
November 5–6

George Porter had a new nickname for himself. "The Invisible Man."

The more crowded the mountain became, the less people noticed him. He was one of a thousand long-haired punks, one of a thousand dirty faces—all lost, all waiting for something to happen, all the same. It was a trip. So he blended in and disappeared. He didn't have to hide in treetops anymore, like a chimpanzee. He didn't have to creep through the dirt and under-brush, like a snake. He could act like a person again. There was nothing to be scared of.

He was *safe*.

It took a while for him to relax, though. A couple of weeks. But weirdly enough, the black smog in the sky eased his mind. Without the sun there were no visions. No pain. No unseen hands smacking him upside the neck. He was comfortable for once. Normal, even. Just like he had been when the *world* was normal. The pull was gone: the wrenching tug in his gut that dragged him toward Babylon. He'd almost forgotten about all those trippy flashes—the baby with one brown eye and one green, the cliff overlooking the ocean. . . .

27

Almost.

It was kind of funny. He didn't know *why* the sun had anything to do with the visions. He just knew it did. He didn't particularly give a crap, either. No, he had only two concerns. He had to find Julia and get her the hell away from this mountain. He also had to stay alive long enough to do it, which meant steering clear of those chicks in black robes.

But they'll never find me.

At first he'd kept hidden, lurking in the woods near the campfires, listening in on scraps of conversation for the telltale signs: a girl with a strange accent, maybe; a girl who talked about "getting her kicks while she could." But if the Demon's sick little posse of helpers was still hanging around the mountain, he didn't know about it.

Maybe they had gone to be with Ariel . . . or Lilith, or whoever the hell she was. Or maybe they had blended in too, like him. They *had* to, right? They sure couldn't risk dancing around and chanting in some weird language, blabbing about how they had suckered Harold Wurf. They were too smart. It was the greatest con game in history, and every single kid on earth was being played.

Every kid except the Invisible Man.

"Did you hear the news?" somebody was yelling. "He's here! The Chosen One is here!"

Here we go again, George thought, scowling.

He crouched by a raging bonfire, mushed in with a couple of dozen others who were trying to stay warm in the long, long night on the cold mountain.

He didn't particularly feel like moving. Not for a false alarm. Every few hours or so somebody would start hollering about how "the Chosen One" was finally here. It made him sick. The kids reminded him of a bunch of five-year-olds who were waiting for a birthday clown to show up.

But before he knew it, everybody was jumping up.

"There he is! He's coming this way!"

"Come on," a girl urged, grabbing George's hand and yanking him out of the sea of scrambling legs. "He's right over there. . . ."

"I've come to heal you!" a voice bellowed over the shouts and scuffling and roaring flames. "The time is almost upon us! You are my Chosen People!"

Harold. No doubt. It was the same smarmy, game-show-style rap. George shook free of the girl's hand. Hot excitement surged through his body. *Julia.* He craned his neck, but all he saw was a sea of heads. *Damn.* He needed to get a better look. Because if Harold was here—really *here*—then Julia wouldn't be far behind.

In a flash he ducked through the crowd, shoving his way into the woods. His breath came fast. His eyes darted around the shadowy tangle of trees. He needed to find a good one to climb. . . . *Right here.* Yeah. The trunk was thick; the pine needles would offer good cover in case anybody's eyes wandered. He jumped and grabbed one of the branches, then swung his legs around the trunk—shimmying up it like a monkey. The rough bark scraped his palms and thighs, but he didn't care. He was getting pretty good at this.

Up and up he went, as easily as if he were climbing a ladder . . . until he reached a broad limb and perched himself high above the firelit trail.

Holy crap. There he is.

Harold still looked exactly the same. Same lame-ass ponytail, same phony smile. He was even wearing that stupid white lab coat. George shook his head. It was almost comical. Everybody was swirling around Harold, like toilet water around a drain. Even from where George was sitting, even with branches blocking his view and the dim firelight, he could tell that Harold was giving all the chicks the eye. The Chosen One hadn't changed much, had he?

George gripped the tree tightly and leaned forward. His eyes narrowed as he searched the shadowy crowd for Julia's familiar brown curls, that willowy frame. . . . But she was nowhere to be seen.

Linda was there, though. Right next to Harold. She had her arm around him. George smirked. Now, *that* was funny. The poor dope had no idea that his trusty blond sidekick was really one of Lilith's crew. George was half tempted to spit on them. Where the hell was Julia? The tree swayed in the bitter wind. This wasn't good. Maybe she was lagging behind or something—

"I've come to give you a message!" Harold suddenly cried.

The crowd fell silent. George held his breath.

"In two weeks' time a momentous event will take place," Harold proclaimed. "The cloud above us will disappear. The Demon's hold on our planet will be broken. And on that day I want you all to start gathering

30

on the western slope." He pumped a fist in the air. "There I will grant you eternal life!"

A wild cheer erupted from the swarm of kids.

I think I'm gonna barf, George thought. How could people be so thick? Pathetic didn't even begin to describe it—especially because Harold's skills were obviously slipping. Those lines sounded as if they were lifted from some cheesy commercial. Then again, Harold didn't really need to try as hard to impress anymore. People already believed in him. He could say whatever he pleased.

Well. There was no point in getting pissed about it. George had to move. Quickly. He had to get Harold alone—away from Linda—and find out where Julia was. Yeah. The key was hiding from Linda. Hopefully she thought he was dead, nothing more than a black stain on the floor of Harold's cellar back in Texas.

Because if she found out the truth, he wouldn't be alive for much longer.

A full day passed before Linda finally left Harold's side. It felt like a full day to George, anyway—it was impossible to know in the constant darkness. She had to find a place to go to the bathroom. It figured. There were some things that people had to do alone, no matter what. George knew he didn't have much time. Not that he needed much. He had to find Julia and get out: That was his plan. Oh, yeah. And to tell Harold that he *wasn't* the Chosen One. That Harold was in fact a loser. That he was a pawn who was about to get whacked. *That* would be fun.

George had been thinking a lot about how he

31

would break the news. He'd been imagining the scene pretty much nonstop as he followed Linda and Harold up and down the mountain trails, safely hidden in the darkness and the crowds of those dumb kids. . . .

And now he had his chance.

Harold had broken off from the mob and was talking to a group of four girls in a clearing on the side of the path—a good distance from the torches and flashlights. *Perfect*. George crept through the woods, sneaking around the rest of the crowd until he was right behind Harold, maybe only five feet away.

The girls eyed him curiously.

"Hey, Harold," George whispered, crouching low to the ground. "Who's got your back?"

Harold whirled around—and nearly fell over.

His face whitened. His jaw dropped. His eyes bulged. He was actually *shaking*.

"You!" he gasped.

"Me," George answered. He grinned, then took a quick look around, scanning for Linda. She was nowhere to be seen. He stood up straight and beckoned to Harold with a quick, jerky wave of his hand. "Come on, buddy. We're taking a walk."

Harold didn't budge. "B-but . . . ," he stammered, shaking his head.

The girls shifted on their feet, exchanging nervous glances.

"Now," George barked. He pounced forward and seized Harold by the arm, then dragged him back into the dense, black forest. "I don't have time."

"Hey!" one of the girls yelled. "Don't—"

"Shut up!" George snarled. "He'll be right back. Don't sweat it."

Harold stumbled along beside him. He didn't say a word. George was pretty amazed, actually. The guy wasn't putting up any kind of fight at all. He was a total pushover. But then again, he probably thought that George was a ghost or something. He'd also never been physically confronted before—at least as far as George knew.

"I . . . I thought you were dead," Harold finally croaked. "How the hell did you—"

"*I'm* asking the questions," George growled, swatting branches out of the way with his free hand. He couldn't see a damn thing. He glanced over his shoulder, but nobody was following them. Good. The voices and lights were far away.

He jerked to a stop and looked Harold in the face. "Where's Julia?"

But Harold just kept shaking his head. "George, tell me what's going on," he whispered, voice trembling. "How did you get here? You vaporized in my basement—"

"You mean, you *thought* I vaporized in your basement," George countered. He chuckled. "Surprise, surprise. Even a genius like you can be taken, huh Harold?"

Harold's forehead wrinkled. "But—but . . . how did you *do* it?"

"It was pretty easy, man," George said with a shrug. "I just dipped my clothes in some rotten pig feed and snuck through that hole in the floor. Anybody could have done it."

"Impossible," Harold muttered. He sounded as if he were talking to himself. "There's no way anybody could have—"

"Wrong," George mumbled. He shoved Harold, sending him staggering back against a tree. "Now, where's Julia?"

Harold straightened. Even in the darkness George could see that his face was twisted with rage. "Don't touch me!" he shouted. "Don't you *ever* touch me!"

"Believe me, I don't want to," George said. "So answer my question."

"She's dead."

Dead. George's breath caught in his throat. The word echoed through his brain. *Dead.* It wasn't possible, couldn't be possible. . . .

"You're lying," he whispered.

"Why would I lie about Julia? I wanted her as much as you did, remember?"

You bastard! George bristled. Rage flashed through him. He clenched his fingers into tight fists and drew one of them back. "I'm giving you one more chance," he stated, his words sounding empty even to himself. "Tell me where she is."

"Or what?" Harold groaned. "Or you'll hit me? All I need to do is raise my voice, and a hundred kids will tear you to shreds in a matter of seconds."

George's arm faltered for a moment. He could feel his confidence slipping away. What was he thinking? Harold was right. Every single kid on this mountain would *gladly* beat George to a pulp for Harold's sake.

"Look, George, I don't *know* what happened to her," Harold said after a moment. "All I know is that the Demon poisoned her mind, and she disappeared in an earthquake. That's the truth. It's safe to assume that she died."

"What do you mean, the Demon poisoned her mind?" George demanded.

Harold laughed. "She became a heretic like you. And all heretics die sooner or later. Didn't you learn anything in the Promised Land?"

George drew in a ragged breath, hope flickering inside him. Julia had escaped. Harold hadn't *seen* her die. Right? So there was a chance she was alive. Best of all, she had finally seen Harold for who he was. She had finally realized that George was telling her the truth.

"Okay, Harold," George whispered. "Okay."

He took a step back and shot a glance toward the clearing. Still no sign of trouble. He knew what he had to do. He had to hightail it back to Babylon. Because if Julia had escaped in time, her visions would have brought her there. His heart squeezed. He couldn't believe it. She might have been there a long time already—unless the cloud kept her from finding her way.

"I'm gonna split now," he said.

Harold smiled. "You can still join me, you know," he offered. "There's still time to repent. You see . . . as much as I'd like to hate you, George, I don't. The Chosen One doesn't hate. And you're pretty smart for a sniveling twerp, you know that? I don't think anyone else could have fooled me into thinking that they were dead."

George rolled his eyes. "You're not the Chosen

35

One, Harold," he said with a moan. Funny. He'd been looking forward to saying that for days, *weeks* even— but now he was too impatient and fed up to appreciate the moment.

"So say the heretics," Harold replied.

"No—so says the Chosen One. The *real* Chosen One. I've met her. The Demon, too."

Harold laughed again. "Oh, you *have?*"

"Look, man, I'm trying to help you," George snapped. "You're a chump, Harold, and you don't even know it. The Demon *wants* you to believe that you're the Chosen One. All those miracles you performed? The Demon pulled those off. Like when you thought you got rid of the locusts back at your farm—"

"That's quite enough, George," Harold interrupted coldly. "I don't need to be lectured by you. You're not *that* smart."

George shook his head. "Whatever."

"Harold?" Linda's voice rang faintly through the trees. "Harold, where are you?"

Uh-oh. Time to bail. George took a few steps back. "I'd watch out for Linda if I was you. She's playing you, man. You and your whole freaking flock."

But Harold just waved his hand dismissively. "Go on. Get out of here. You'll die soon enough. Just like all the rest of the heretics."

"Harold?" Linda called.

"Over here!" Harold answered.

There was a rustling in the trees. George's pulse picked up a beat.

"You're gonna remember me," he whispered, edging deeper into the forest. "You're gonna remember what I said. But by then it'll be too late."

Before Harold could reply, George turned and fled—vanishing into the tangled abyss of the wilderness. He'd gotten what he needed. Hell. If Harold really wanted to stick around, that was *his* problem.

CHAPTER FOUR

**Washington Institute of Technology,
Babylon, Washington
November 7–10**

"Ariel, are you sure you don't want to come with us?" Leslie murmured.

Ariel shook her head. She knew she should help Leslie and the other kids at WIT deal with the remains of Sarah and Jezebel. They were in *her* house, after all. Besides, she knew it would provide some relief, a sense of finality . . . what was the word? Closure. But she couldn't do it. She couldn't get herself to leave the campus—or even to move. She'd been sitting on the lawn outside the communications lab for what seemed like years . . . just sitting. Even *thinking* about that bloody scene in the front hall was enough to start her bawling for hours on end. No. There was no way she could go home. She might not ever be able to go there again.

"What are you going to do with the bodies?" Ariel whispered, staring blankly into the darkness.

Leslie sighed. "We'll bury Sarah near that cliff overlooking the ocean," she said. "It's a beautiful spot. I think she would have liked it."

Ariel nodded. "What about Jezebel?" she asked.

"Jezebel?" Leslie's face twisted into a sneer.

"Don't worry. We're gonna dump her in the sewer, where she belongs."

The days plodded by in a haze. Ariel didn't even know how she felt. She knew she should have been happy—at least *partially* happy. Everybody else at WIT was celebrating. That was an understatement, actually. All the hundreds of Visionaries and stragglers and hangers-on were whooping it up as if they'd just been freed from slavery or something. And in a way, they *had* been freed: from their visions, from the Demon, from the prophecies . . . even from the plague. Ariel just had to take one whiff of the rank cauldron of boiling turnip bulbs to be reminded of *that*.

Sarah had saved every one of these people. It was all she'd ever wanted to do.

So why can't you get psyched? Ariel kept asking herself. *Sarah would have wanted you to join in the fun, right?*

She spent most of the time sitting alone—staring at all the smiling faces around the various campfires, trying to figure out what they were getting that she wasn't. Weren't they just a little bit upset by the fact that the Chosen One was *dead?* That they'd just buried her? Maybe not. After all, none of them even knew her very well . . . none of them except Ariel. Most of them had been afraid of Sarah, in fact. They had kept their distance. She was more of a figurehead than a real person to them, somebody who inspired awe and fear and gratitude, but very little warmth.

She was a real person to Ariel, though.

No, she was more than that. She was a *friend*.

At least Leslie seemed to be making an effort to get the kids to remember Sarah for who she really was. It was funny: Leslie had never even *liked* Sarah. But true to her word, she spent every spare second hopping from one little clique to the next, telling of how Sarah had sacrificed herself so that the rest of the world could carry on. Leslie was just doing what she did best, of course—which was socializing. Only now she had a *cause*, a purpose. She was like some kind of traveling preacher. She'd even gone so far as to suggest that the freakish black cloud in the sky was a sign that the entire planet was still suffering for the Chosen One's death. It was incredibly intense—and totally out of character . . . and, well, just plain *sweet*.

I bet I know why Leslie is so gung ho, Ariel thought. *She feels bad about fighting with me over Sarah.*

But she kept that thought to herself. Motives didn't matter. What mattered was that people were finally learning the truth about the Chosen One.

"Believers! The Chosen One is coming! He heals all those in his path! Wait for him on the western slope of Mount Rainier! There you will receive his blessing—"

Leslie flicked a switch on the dust-covered ham radio. The annoying voice fell silent. She glanced at Ariel.

"See?" she asked.

"See what?" Ariel mumbled, slouching against a

41

wall. She was tense, restless. She didn't like spending time in this building. It conjured up too many painful ghosts. Like the memory of Ariel's own brother. Trevor had *died* in this place. So had her ex-boyfriend, Brian Landau. So had a lot of other people. She herself had almost died. . . . *Ugh*. She felt as if the walls of the dank, candlelit laboratory were shrinking—squeezing the air out, suffocating her. The stench of the plague antidote drifted in from the hall. She pinched her nostrils between two fingers. They'd heard this same broadcast before. More than once. A lot more. It was old news.

"Somebody's still out there, pretending to be the Chosen One," Leslie stated. "Doesn't that piss you off?"

Ariel shrugged. "A little. But there isn't much we can do about it." She stood up straight, keeping her hand clamped over her nose. Her voice sounded flat and nasal. "Listen, Leslie, I'm gonna go—"

"Come on!" Leslie cried. "This is important!"

"Why?" Ariel moaned. Her hand slipped from her face. She didn't mean to be bitchy, but she couldn't help it. She was exhausted. "Whoever this guy is, he isn't going to get very far pretending that he's the Chosen One. Anyway, Sarah said that the radio messages were all part of a trap set by the Demon's helpers. And the Demon is dead, right? So I don't think we have anything to worry about. Can't we just get on with our lives?"

Leslie shook her head. "But this . . . this *guy* is pretending to be Sarah!" She sputtered the words in a frenzy. "It's like he's spitting on Sarah's grave. Didn't we promise to tell as many people as possible about what she did for us? Didn't we promise to make her memory live forever? This guy is sabotaging that. *Sarah* wouldn't have wanted this to happen. She would have wanted us to go down to Mount Rainier and kick some ass."

Ariel managed a tired grin. "I don't know, Leslie. Sarah wasn't really the ass-kicking type. I think *you* want to go down there. And I totally understand that. But I also honestly think if we ignore this guy, he'll end up going away."

"Oh, please." Leslie rolled her eyes, but she was smiling, too. "You sound like my mom. We owe it to Sarah. We owe it to ourselves. It's the *least* we can do."

"Yeah, but . . ." Ariel bit her lip, hesitating.

As much as she hated to admit it, she was a little scared of leaving town, of going someplace unfamiliar. She didn't know exactly why. There was nothing to fear. Sarah had killed the Demon; she'd cured the plague. . . .

"What is it?" Leslie asked.

She sighed. "I don't know. It's just . . . the prophecies for this month said that the Demon's servants are gonna lead the False Prophet to his own doom. So maybe the scroll was talking about these radio messages. Maybe this stuff is *supposed* to happen."

Leslie's smile faltered. "But the prophecies can't come true anymore," she murmured. "That's why Sarah . . ." She didn't finish.

"I know, I know," Ariel mumbled. "Look, I don't even know what I'm talking about. It's just that I have this weird feeling inside. I can't explain it." She drew in her breath. "I can't help thinking that something bad is gonna happen soon. I've felt that way for a long time. And I *still* feel it. Even now."

Their eyes met for a moment.

Leslie nodded, her face softening.

And then a miraculous thing occurred . . . a sense of warm relief filled an empty space in Ariel's body. She suddenly realized that she had never admitted that to anyone. Never told anyone of her nagging fear—not even Sarah. Why had she been so reluctant to be honest? It was as if an invisible connection had been reestablished—as if she remembered all at once why she and Leslie were best friends in the first place. They could *communicate*. They didn't have to hide anything from each other. Maybe that was why they'd wasted so much time bickering these past few months. They'd been keeping too many secrets.

"It's okay, Ariel," Leslie whispered. "Really. I know why you don't want to go. But if the False Prophet is still out there, then maybe the Demon's helpers are, too. There's a chance that they don't even know Jezebel is dead. I mean, nobody could know about *any* of this stuff unless somebody from Babylon told them, right?"

Ariel opened her mouth, but no words would come. She stared down at the ham radio.

Leslie was right. The Demon's helpers might very well be carrying on as if Jezebel were still alive. That would help to explain the broadcast. The truth of the matter was that neither Ariel nor Leslie really knew anything. They were still struggling—blindly, in the dark—relying on their gut instincts and what little Sarah had told them.

There's so much we don't know.

Maybe she should read Sarah's notebook again. Really *read* it—not just skim it. The thought of it frightened her, but the answers to those questions must be hidden in there somewhere. . . .

"I've got an idea," Leslie said.

Ariel glanced up at her. "What's that?"

"Why don't you stay here?" Leslie suggested. *"I'll* go down to Mount Rainier. I'll take as many kids as I can with me. We'll show this False Prophet guy what's up, and you take the time to chill and recover. By yourself. I mean . . . I mean, you and Sarah were really tight. This, uh—this has gotta be hard." Her voice caught. She sniffed and turned away. "She was, like, your best friend—"

"You're my best friend," Ariel interrupted clumsily. She looked down again. "You always were. That's why I want you to stay. It could be dangerous to go fight this guy."

Leslie took a deep breath. "I know, Ariel. But I *have* to go. Because I was a bitch to Sarah. I was always—"

"You weren't that bad," Ariel cut in. But she knew she was only trying to make Leslie feel better.

"Yeah, I was," Leslie replied softly. "And maybe . . . I don't know, maybe I was jealous of you guys, like you said. I don't know. All I know is that Sarah was the Chosen One, and I never got a chance to know her or thank her or anything. And I'm gonna make it up to her. *Now.*"

45

Ariel sighed. She didn't try to protest. There was no stopping Leslie; she'd made up her mind. Ariel knew that tone all too well—that stubborn defiance that stated: *I don't care what anybody thinks. I'm gonna do this.* In a way, it was one of the things that Ariel loved most about her. It was like a mirror in which Ariel saw herself.

Without another word Leslie strode to the door—head down, avoiding Ariel's eyes.

"Be careful," Ariel whispered.

Leslie paused with her hand on the doorknob. "I will. You be careful, too."

There was a moment of silence. Ariel held her breath—desperately wishing Leslie would reassure her, crack a joke, smile . . . *anything.*

But she didn't.

She simply closed the door behind her, leaving Ariel in solitude.

November

PART II

November 11-25

Old Pine Mall,
Babylon, Washington
November 11

Caleb Walker had to make a decision. He *hated* making decisions. Especially important ones. Small ones were okay, like: "I'm *not* going to quit smoking." He could deal with those. But usually he preferred to have somebody make his decisions for him. *I think you should do this, Caleb. I think you should do that, Caleb. I think you should do whatever feels good, Caleb. Don't you? Yes. Yes, I do.*

Only this was different. And theoretically, it should have been easy. He could either go to Mount Rainier with Leslie, or he could stay in Babylon with Ariel. It was a simple matter of choosing A or B. Anyway, even if he *didn't* go with Leslie, she wouldn't be gone for long, right?

Right?

I could really use a drink.

That was why he had come back to the mall in the first place—and back to this freakish toy store in particular. He was hoping to scrounge up some booze. Of course, he'd told Ariel and Leslie that he needed to gather some of his "stuff." Sure. What stuff? People didn't even *have* stuff anymore. Just the clothes on their backs and the crap they found as they went along. The girls probably knew he was lying.

It didn't matter, though. He'd stupidly forgotten that all the booze was gone. He and Jezebel had finished all the peppermint schnapps right before she'd ditched him. Too bad. In a way, however, he supposed it served him right. It was divine justice or something. He didn't *deserve* a drink.

He frowned, kicking the empty bottles at his feet. They tinkled loudly on the filthy carpet. Man, this place was a mess. Spent candles were everywhere. Big drops of wax hung from all the shelves, frozen in space like icicles. It was a miracle he hadn't burned the entire mall to the ground. He couldn't believe that he'd actually *lived* here for a month—lying around in a drunken stupor, playing with little plastic figures . . . playing with Jezebel. He shuddered.

No, *she* had played with him.

Even just one lousy sip of warm beer or something—

Okay, okay. He wasn't going to cry over it. Leslie would be here soon. She wanted to get on the road. It was a good thing he was sober. Wasn't it? He was *himself,* unaltered and clearheaded. He stole a quick peek at one of the fun house mirrors hanging on the back wall.

Bad idea.

He didn't *look* like himself. He looked like a big fat midget with a four-foot-tall pinhead.

An unpleasant, nervous spasm flickered through his stomach. Staring at his distorted reflection, he couldn't help thinking about the very first time Jezebel had brought him here. It was July Fourth. His favorite holiday. Beer, beer, beer. Only he couldn't find any. So Jezebel had gotten him drunk and showed him these mirrors. Then she went off on some weird rant about how the mirrors reminded her of Ariel because "you think you're looking at one thing, but you're really looking at another" . . . or something like that. He shook his head. Jezebel had been acting as if *Ariel* was the phony. As if *Ariel* was the Demon. Jezebel was pretty damn convincing. He'd believed her, right?

The Demon.

Caleb turned the word around in his mind. Jezebel was a Demon. Sarah was a Chosen One. What did it mean? Nobody knew. Neither of those labels even seemed *real*—especially now, after Jezebel and Sarah had mowed each other down in a gunfight. Did the prophecies predict that they would die like that? Like gang members in a meaningless turf war? Caleb was never a religious guy . . . but still, it didn't seem *right.*

Then again, he didn't even know if any of this stuff had anything to do with religion. It was more like—what? Magic? Mystery? Something from a cable TV special, hosted by that guy from *Star Trek?*

The strangest part of all was that it involved *him.* Caleb Walker. A scrub from Seattle. Why? Why had *he* been lucky enough (or unlucky enough) to meet the Demon and the Chosen One? What if he had lived in New York City, or LA, or someplace like Australia? Then he wouldn't have had to deal with any of this. Life would have been a hell of a lot easier.

But maybe everyplace on earth had their own Demon and Chosen One. Maybe there were thousands of kids just like him—and like Jezebel and Sarah, too—scattered across the globe.

Yeah. *That* would be a lot easier to swallow. It would mean that he wasn't so special.

He hung his head. Who was he kidding? He wasn't special. He knew it. He'd always known it. He just happened to be caught up in the wrong place at the wrong time—

There were footsteps in the hall.

Crap. So much for making a decision before Leslie arrived. He turned around, peering at the darkened door through an aisle of boxes and masks.

"Caleb?" Leslie called.

"In here," he answered quietly.

She appeared in the doorway. He lowered his eyes. Just a glimpse of that black miniskirt was enough to bring on that familiar feeling . . . guilt. Good old guilt. It was like a close friend now. A constant buddy.

"Did you get your stuff?" she asked.

He laughed. "Yeah. Yeah, I got it."

"What's so funny?"

He shook his head. "Nothing." He glanced up at her. *Damn,* she was beautiful. Even after all the long months of fighting for survival, she managed to maintain her looks—when everyone else had gone the way of haggard bums. Like him. But then, personal grooming had never been much of a priority.

"You know, Caleb . . . I've been thinking," she said.

52

Uh-oh. Thinking was always a bad sign.

"I don't think you should come with me," she stated. "I think you should stay here with Ariel. If you don't, she's gonna be all alone. Everybody in town is making the trip. And after all she's been through . . ." She took a deep breath. "Ariel needs you, Caleb. Now's the perfect time for you guys to start over."

Caleb blinked a few times. He had no idea what to say. Part of him was relieved, of course—first of all, that a decision had been made *for* him; second, that he wouldn't have to help pick a fight with some guy at Mount Rainier.

On the other hand, he couldn't help but feel a little shafted. He knew he should be cool with Leslie's leaving. Ariel *was* supposed to be his girlfriend . . . but still, he and Leslie had shared something, too. More than once. Recently. He couldn't ignore the unpleasant sensation in his chest—the sensation that he was *losing* someone.

"What about us?" he found himself asking.

Jeez. His face grew hot. Why did he say that? He should just keep his mouth shut—

"Look, Caleb . . . I know that there's something between us," she murmured. "We both know it. But whatever it is, it's not as important as what you've got with Ariel. We both know that, too. I mean, the whole reason you locked yourself away with Jezebel that whole time was for *Ariel's* sake. Not mine. You love that girl, Caleb. So, I think—well, I think that *we* should start over, too. Officially. As friends."

Caleb swallowed. "But what about . . ." He didn't

finish. He was going to ask: *But what about when we hid in here and made out two weeks ago?*

"None of the stuff that happened in the past really matters," Leslie said, as if reading his mind. "I mean—like, when we fooled around in here, it wasn't really a sexual kind of thing. It was more . . . I don't know. We were both lonely. We were both scared. You know?"

Yeah. Caleb *did* know. He'd had those same exact thoughts himself.

But knowing all that didn't make him feel any better about it—*or* about letting Leslie go.

Leslie sighed. She stepped quickly down the aisle and took Caleb's hands in her own. "Look," she whispered. "I'm not sorry about what happened. I'm not sorry about any of it. But we should move on. It'll be our little secret. I think we should try to look at the whole event like an old photo or something. It belongs to us, and we can take it out and look at it whenever we want. But it's part of the past. We can't make it happen again."

He nodded, staring down at their intertwined fingers. He couldn't bring himself to meet her gaze. She was right; he knew she was right. It was over between them. This very conversation clinched it.

"I want you to do me a favor, Caleb," Leslie said after a moment.

"What's that?"

"Keep an eye on Ariel, all right? Try to take her mind off Sarah. I mean, don't let her spend all her time staring at Sarah's old notebook and things. None of that prophecy stuff matters anymore, anyway." She let go of his hands. "Ariel needs to start living her life again. She needs a break. We *all* need a break."

You got that right, Caleb answered silently.

Neither of them spoke for several seconds. For some reason, Caleb's throat felt constricted. His eyes were smarting. What was his problem? Was he sad that Leslie was leaving? Was he scared? He didn't even know anymore.

Finally Leslie turned toward the door. "I better get going. People are waiting for me."

"Okay," he whispered.

She glanced over her shoulder. "See you later, Caleb."

"See ya."

She padded back down the hallway.

"Do you really think that going after this False Prophet guy is gonna solve anything?" Caleb called after her.

"Yeah," she answered. She didn't bother turning around. "I really do."

CHAPTER SIX

Babylon,
Washington
November 12–16

November 12 (I think it's the 12th)

So. Here I go again.

How many times have I radically altered my life in the past year? A hundred? A million? I can't even keep track anymore.

But I should expect a lot of changes. Change is normal. It's healthy, even. I should just deal. As Sarah would say, "Kay sera, sera." (I don't think I spelled that right, but who cares? It's not like Mr. Wilson is gonna rise up from the dead and grade this. On the other hand, maybe he will. Like I said, i'll deal.)

Anyway, Babylon is like a ghost

town. Caleb and I are the only people who decided to stay. Everybody else followed Leslie down to Mount Rainier. Everybody. Nobody even stuck around to make the antidote anymore. That big vat is sitting on the lawn at WIS on top of a bunch of burnt wood. There's garbage all over the place. It's gross. It reminds me of the way my yard used to look after a party.

At least it doesn't reek anymore.

November 13

These past couple of days have been so strange. The empty town is starting to freak me out. I went back to my house for the first time since Jezebel and Sarah died. I'm surprised I could do it. Maybe I'm finally coming to terms with Sarah's death. It was so weird, walking through that empty house, just Caleb and me. We didn't have much to say. I guess it brought back a lot of memories for both of us.

Why do I still feel afraid? Is it that black cloud? I don't know. All I know is that I really want everyone to come back. Especially Leslie.

Maybe I should have gone with them. Maybe I was just being a wimp. Leslie's doing this whole thing for Sarah, and she wasn't even friends with her. I'm the one who should be honoring her in some way.

But saying "should have" never got me anywhere, right?

November 14

I don't believe it   I'm actually happy. Not just plain happy, either. I don't think I've ever been as happy as I am right now. I feel like I could sing or something. Okay, maybe not. I've got a pretty lousy voice.

Caleb is asleep beside me. We just had the most amazing talk. He told me all this stuff he was keeping inside. Like about how he spent the past month driving himself crazy, trying to figure out a way to prove that I wasn't the Demon. Apparently he even spent a lot of time hanging with Jezebel, trying to catch her off guard. How did he do it? He's so brave. He must have been scared out of his mind. I know I would have been.

He also told me how guilty he feels about fooling around with Leslie back in April. I told him it didn't matter, but he said he regretted it, and he's been true to me ever since. He's psyched that we're alone, just the two of us. He said it's like a romantic honeymoon or something. I can't believe it! I sort of broke down and cried, and he hugged me for a really long time. We didn't even fool around. We didn't even kiss. We just . . . I don't know. Bonded.

I don't know how he can sleep right now. I'm all wired and full of energy, like I just drank eight cups of coffee. Maybe it's late at night. Who knows? As long as Caleb is here with me, I don't even care if I ever see the sun again.

November 15

Another amazing conversation. It's funny. Now I'm glad everybody's gone. Who would have guessed? I think I might actually be falling in love . . . with somebody I'm already in love with. (I know that doesn't make sense, but I'm in one of those sappy moods. I'll probably puke when I read this tomorrow.)

We talked a lot about growing up. For the first time I was able to talk about what happened to Mom. The accident. I didn't want to scream or cry or hurt myself. Caleb just makes me feel so comfortable, so at ease. It's like I've been this big shaken soda can, with all this stuff just waiting to explode out of me, and he popped the lid. Kaboom!

Maybe I'm starting to accept Mom's death. Caleb kept reminding me about how Trevor forgave me for it. That helps.

We also talked about Sarah a little. I guess I wanted to talk about her more than he did. He said he missed her, and not much else. He must still be in shock.

November 16

Today I decided to flip through Sarah's diary, just for the hell of it. I feel like there are still some questions I need to answer. Sarah did ask me to try to crack the code. As if I even have a chance.

That feeling hasn't gone away, either:

the doom or whatever. At least it's not as strong as it was before. I don't think it is, anyway. But . . . I don't even know. Something isn't quite right. That black cloud is still in the sky.

I didn't look at the notebook for long. It bummed Caleb out. He said he didn't want to think about that stuff, magic or prophecies or anything. He just wants to forget about it for a while. I can totally relate to that.

But sooner or later I'll take a good look at what Sarah wrote. Maybe I'll wait until Caleb is asleep—he doesn't have to know about it. It's just something I have to do. I owe it to Sarah. This will be my way of honoring her, of remembering her. The other kids can chase down the False Prophet, and I'll crack the code.

Just like she asked me to do.

**Highway 90,
near Spokane, Washington
November 18**

The highway was very smooth, but even the slightest bump would send a twinge of pain shooting through Julia Morrison's taut belly. She lay flat on her back in the backseat of the Range Rover—eyes closed, hands over her bulging womb, drenched in perspiration. *How much longer? Are we there yet?*

Lord help me.

At least she wouldn't have to endure the torture forever. Just a few more days. She and Bob and Ted had been driving for a long time now. This strange town—this place called Babylon where the Chosen One and Demon had appeared—it couldn't be *that* far off. They had already crossed the state line, after all. Anyway, there was a chance she'd have the baby before they got there. Nine months were almost up. She had to keep reminding herself of that. It was the only way she could keep going. The baby was due any minute now. Any minute—

The car bounced.

She cried out in agony, arching her back. Why was she hurting so badly? Was this normal? Was her child in some kind of danger? She almost wished she

65

could talk to Harold—just to ask him some questions. No . . . she didn't wish that. But still, Harold Wurf was probably the closest thing to a doctor left on earth. And *that* scared her more than anything. There was nobody left to give her advice, nobody to treat her baby in case of injury or sickness. She was on her own.

"Sorry," Bob muttered from the driver's seat. "The road's kinda messed up around here. All these wrecks. The highway's really jammed—"

"So why don't you ease off the gas a little?" Ted interrupted.

The car began to slow.

Julia struggled to breathe evenly. Bob and Ted. Her knights in shining yellow raincoats. The boys who'd heard of a mysterious pregnant girl—the girl who carried the baby that would defeat the Demon. Was she even the one? It didn't seem possible. And she still didn't know if she could trust these guys. She didn't even know their last names. All she knew was that they were going very far out of their way to take her back to a place they didn't want to be . . . and the longer they drove, the more tension there seemed to be between them.

Her eyelids remained tightly shut. She wished she could say something, do something to ease the tension—but it took every ounce of her energy just to keep from crying out. Maybe they should just stop for the night. If it *was* night.

"How're you doin' back there?" Bob asked.

Julia licked her dry lips. "I . . . I think I need a little break," she croaked. "If that's okay."

"Sure," Bob replied. He sounded worried. She could hear him shifting in his seat. "Are you all right?"

"Yeah," she lied. "Just a little tired—"

"Bob, watch out!" Ted shrieked.

The tires squealed. Julia was instantly thrown forward. *Help!* In a panic she thrust out her hands to soften the blow—and her palms smacked the vinyl seat backs. She tumbled to the car floor. The next moment she was bouncing around like a pinball. A terrible burning sensation stabbed through her spine. *Stop it! My baby. My baby—*

The car lurched to a halt.

"My God." Bob gasped.

Ted squirmed around to get a good look at her, brushing his long black hair out of his face. "Julia? Are you okay?"

She couldn't answer. She couldn't *breathe*. What had happened? She lay still, mushed in the chasm between the front and backseats, gazing up at him in terror.

"Those *idiots*," Bob growled. "I'm really sorry." He rolled down the window. "Hey! What are you doing in the middle of the road?"

"What's going on?" Julia managed.

Ted reached out and extended a hand for her to grab. "We almost ran some people over," he mumbled. "Here. I'll help you back up."

She took his arm. With a grunt he gingerly eased her back into the seat.

How did she feel? She couldn't tell. She exhaled cautiously and patted her stomach. It didn't hurt *too* much . . . but maybe she shouldn't think about it. No. Better to focus on something else. She leaned forward and peered out the windshield into the darkness. Several kids were approaching the car. Their faces looked pale in the white glare of the headlights.

"Sorry!" one of them called. "We just weren't expecting to see any traffic, you know? All this junk out here—"

"Where are you coming from?" Bob interrupted.

Julia bit her lip. There were a *lot* of kids. Maybe a dozen or more.

"We're coming from Babylon," a boy answered.

Babylon?

"Hey—is that *you*, Bob?"

Bob stuck his head out the window. "David? What are you guys doing out here?"

"What are *you* doing out here?" the boy replied. "I thought you went home."

Baffled, Julia stuck her head between the two front seats. The car was surrounded now.

"What's going on?" she whispered to Ted. "You know these people?"

Ted shrugged. "Some of them."

"We *did* go home," Bob told the boy. He jerked his thumb back toward Julia. "But we found the girl those Visionaries were talking about. You know, the pregnant one—"

"No, no," Julia interrupted. She didn't want anybody to know anything about her. For all she knew, these strangers were connected to Harold, or to the Demon—or they were just a gang of thugs who wouldn't think twice about killing her. Anything was possible. All these months of brutal living had taught her one thing: Be suspicious of everyone. *Everyone.* No exceptions. She had to act like George. *He* had never trusted a soul . . . except her.

"What's the matter?" Bob asked. He glanced back at her.

Julia quickly withdrew her head, slouching down in an attempt to hide behind the seat. "Don't tell them my name," she whispered.

"Who's in there?" the boy asked. He squinted through the back window.

"Uh . . . nobody," Bob mumbled awkwardly. "So why did you guys leave?"

The boy sighed. "'Cause it's over."

"What do you mean?"

"The Chosen One and the Demon are dead. The whole town's deserted. . . ."

Julia's jaw dropped. *Dead?* That couldn't be right. How could the Chosen One be dead? The Chosen One was a savior. She couldn't die. Anyway, Julia had *seen* the Chosen One in her visions. Not face-to-face, of course. But she'd spoken to her. True, she hadn't had any visions since the cloud had blocked the sun, but that didn't mean . . .

". . . Everybody else went off to find some guy named Harold Wurf," the boy was saying. "They're gonna kill him."

"Harold Wurf?" Julia cried, bolting upright.

"Yeah." The boy poked his head through the window. His hair was cropped short, like Bob's—and his face was dirty, cut with craggy lines that made him look a lot older than he sounded. There was a scar on his right cheek. His eyes were cold. "The Chosen One told us that Harold Wurf was the False Prophet from the scroll. Why? You heard of him?"

Don't admit to anything. "No—no," Julia stammered. "No, I haven't. . . ."

The boy's hard gaze bore down upon her. She edged back in the seat. She had to *think.* Fear and bewilderment were starting to fog her mind. She felt as if she were swimming upstream against some impossible current. *The False Prophet from the scroll . . .* What scroll? If the Demon was dead, then what did her visions mean? She thought she was supposed to help *kill* the Demon. Wasn't she?

"What's wrong?" Ted asked.

Julia's eyes darted around the car. Everybody was staring at her.

"There must be some kind of mistake," she whispered.

The boy raised his eyebrows. "How's that?"

"How do you know the Chosen One is dead?" she choked out.

"Because I helped bury her," the boy answered flatly. "We took her body out of that girl Ariel's house and laid her to rest near a cliff overlooking the ocean."

Good Lord. Julia's stomach twisted. A cliff overlooking the ocean . . . George had seen a place like that in his visions.

So maybe the Chosen One *was* dead. Maybe George had seen himself on that cliff because he was doomed to die, too. Or maybe he was supposed to go there, but he had died before his visions could come

70

to pass. Either way, it didn't matter. She felt a sudden, grim certainty that this boy was telling the truth, that *her* visions would never come to pass . . . that she was too late. It was no wonder she'd stopped feeling the pull westward. The pull no longer served a purpose. The battle had already been fought—without her.

"Look, I don't know what you've heard, but this is how it is," the boy said. "The Chosen One is gone. Why do you think it's been dark out for so long? It's like the whole planet is mourning for her. Maybe this cloud will lift, and maybe it won't. All I know is, there isn't much point in hanging around Babylon anymore. We stopped having visions. We stopped feeling the pull. We know how to make the cure for the plague. We should just try to get on with life."

Julia gaped at him. The pain in her belly grew more acute. His voice was somber, resigned—without a trace of hope. It terrified her. How could she get on with life? Was this the world they had inherited: a world without light, a world where bands of depressed teenagers roamed through the ruins of the past, living on a strange cure to stay alive? She wouldn't accept it. No. There had to be something more. . . .

"What do you think, Julia?" Bob asked, glancing back at her.

"I . . . I don't know," she murmured.

"You know what I think?" Ted said. "I think we should turn around and go back to Chicago. Or Springfield, maybe. Someplace where there's electricity. Someplace warm and comfortable where you can have your baby—"

"No," Julia interrupted. "I just . . . I have to keep going. I've come all this way. I'm not going to stop now. I have to see this place for myself."

"I'm tellin' you, there's nothing there," the boy stated.

Bob and Ted exchanged a glance.

"You *really* want to keep going to Babylon?" Bob asked.

Julia nodded, but kept her mouth shut. She couldn't articulate her feelings in any way that would make sense. . . . She only knew that there was nothing to go back to. She *couldn't* turn around now. She knew what lay behind her, back east. She'd been through the abandoned towns and the deserted highways; she'd seen the starving kids with black holes for eyes . . . *animal* eyes. That was no place for a baby. The west could still hold some promise, couldn't it? She wouldn't give up. Even if the Chosen One was dead, even if Julia didn't feel the pull—there was still a chance that something better lay at the end of this road.

"I'm sorry," Bob said with a sigh. "But I'm turning around. I can drop you here if you want. But I'm not gonna drive for nothing. You heard what David said. It's over."

Nothing. Over. Julia winced. The words pierced her like the bullets from a firing squad. She knew then that it wouldn't make a bit of difference *where* her baby was born.

It simply didn't matter. Nothing mattered. Nothing at all.

EIGHT

187 Puget Drive,
Babylon, Washington
November 23

*Tough care mends flaws.
Try to kill nondefensive
spells. Slips affect sins.
Eleven twenty-three ninety-
nine*

Ariel frowned at Sarah's worn notebook, absently
chewing on the end of a ballpoint pen. *Try to kill
nondefensive spells?* What the hell was that supposed
to mean? There was supposed to be a *code* hidden in
here?

Her tired gaze roved over the words again. She
must have looked at this crap for an hour already.
She had a good reason, though.

The date listed—11/23/99—was today.

Well . . . she was pretty sure it was today.

Screw it. Maybe she should just bag the whole
thing. Caleb would be waking up soon, anyway. And
it was pointless to get frustrated. Solving this puzzle
wouldn't do any good. Even if something *was* supposed to happen today, it *couldn't*. The prophecies

were worthless now. She glanced back at the main part of the text, wrinkling her nose. It was a good thing this stuff couldn't come true. It said the Demon was supposed to "eat flesh and drink blood." Ariel always knew Jezebel was a freak—but *cannibalism?* Thank God, she couldn't—

Ariel saw a flash of light out of the corner of her eye.

She looked up from the page. Was something outside?

A little trickle of light had crept through the drawn living room shades, casting a luminous line across the rug. Something *was* out there. A car must have turned onto her street. But who . . . *Leslie*. It had to be. *Yes!* She was back! The light grew brighter, illuminating the entire curtain with a white glow. Leslie must have hitched a ride home.

"Hey, Caleb!" Ariel called, tossing the notebook aside. She shoved the pen into her pocket and hopped up from the couch. "Get your lazy butt out of bed! Somebody's here!"

No answer.

Ariel smirked. He was still passed out upstairs in her bedroom. That boy could sleep through anything. She stood still for a moment, listening for signs of life—but he was obviously dead to the world. It was strange, though. She didn't hear *anything*. No engine, no tires on gravel, no honking horns . . . nothing. If that was a car, it was about the quietest—

What the hell?

The light had grown so bright that she had to squint.

74

It couldn't be coming from a car. No way. The drab white curtain looked as if it had been wired to a high-powered searchlight. For the first time in a long while, she could see the living room in all its grossness: the beer stains on the glass table, the spots on the rug . . . the faint traces of blood that still remained in the front hall.

She held her breath, blinking rapidly.

The light wasn't coming from the street. It was coming from somewhere *above* the street.

"Ariel!" Caleb shouted from upstairs. His voice was breathless. "Ariel!"

She dashed to the front door and threw it open.

Oh, my God.

The sun.

Rays of light beamed down upon her—hot, white, and intense. The shock of it made her stagger. She shielded her eyes with her hand. The black cloud had all but disappeared. Its last few wispy tendrils were melting into nothingness . . . in front of a stunningly blue sky.

The night is over. It's over—

After only a few seconds the glare grew too painful. She closed her eyes. Vibrant red swirls danced under her lids. The heat on her face was like some kind of magic balm—energizing her, healing her. She felt like a moth emerging from a cocoon. She laughed out loud. It was summer. November had never been *this* warm, had it?

Footsteps pounded down the stairwell.

"The sun!" Caleb gasped, skidding to a stop beside her.

"I know," she whispered. "I know. . . ."

"What do you think it means? Do you think Leslie and the others got the False Prophet?"

"Huh?" It was funny: She never would have even *thought* of that. But maybe Caleb was right. Maybe Leslie *had* kicked Harold What's-his-face's ass. And maybe by doing so, she had destroyed the last traces of the Demon and her helpers. The cloud's disappearance was a sign. The Demon was truly gone. It was the dawn of a new day—a new *world*. . . .

All right. She was getting ahead of herself. The sunshine was making her a little giddy. She couldn't wipe the grin from her lips. But it was a possibility, right? *Anything* was a possibility. The scroll said—

The scroll!

"My God," she whispered. Her eyes flew open.

"What?" Caleb asked.

"The prophecies." She turned to him, blinking. Her mouth was suddenly very dry. "Today's date was written in it, right after this really weird part that made no sense."

"It was?" His eyes narrowed. "Why?"

"I . . . I have no idea." Her mind whirled. Could it be that the return of the sun was somehow foretold in those three ridiculous sentences?

Caleb shook his head. "Why—"

But she was already bolting back to the couch. Holding her breath, she snatched up the notebook and ripped through it, searching for the page where Sarah had scribbled some ideas about cracking the code. . . . *There.*

Code Theories

I. Abraham-Translations

A. My interpretation. Code hidden in the way I translate the Hebrew words.

B. Nonsense passages (under every fourth block of text in scroll).

1. Numbers. Connection between dates in English calendar.

2. Primer. Key to deciphering code embedded in words or structure of the scroll itself.

II. Josh and Trevor — Bible Code

A. Equidistant letter sequences.

1. Procedure. String Hebrew words together. Remove breaks and punctuation. Take first letter of string, then skip X amount of letters, take another letter, skip X again.

77

Jeez. Ariel exhaled. Her excitement began to fade. Just looking at this stuff made her woozy. Sarah had been so organized. She was obviously the type of kid who took copious notes in school . . . the type who paid *very* close attention when some burnt-out, underpaid teacher discussed the benefits of a "good outline." Ariel, on the other hand, didn't remember those lessons so well. She'd been busy writing her own notes—most of which concerned the "Loser of the Week" award or how most of the women faculty had more facial hair than Ariel's dad.

Her shoulders sagged. A peculiar, wistful feeling swept over her. She missed Sarah. A lot. Still . . . would she and Sarah have been friends if the world hadn't fallen apart? Probably not. But maybe—in a very strange way—their friendship proved that something positive had come out of all the craziness. At the very least, it proved that Ariel had grown up a lot in the past eleven months. She knew it would sound cheesy if she actually tried to *explain* it, but she no longer concerned herself with the old BS: the random division between "cool" and "uncool." Nobody else did, either. People had learned that there was no point. And that was a good thing.

"Ariel?" Caleb asked.

She glanced up. She hadn't even noticed that he was standing beside her.

"What's going on?" he pressed. He peered over her shoulder at the notebook. "What was supposed to happen today?"

Ariel shook her head. "Uh . . . I don't know. That's what I want to figure out."

Caleb bit his lip. He edged away from her. "Why bother? I mean—"

"I'm going to do this," she stated suddenly.

Yes. The sudden rush of memory and emotion filled her with a new resolve. Her mind wouldn't wander anymore. She'd promised Sarah she would break the code. Besides, it would be fun. Like a puzzle. Sarah had *wanted* this. Cool or uncool, hip or not, Sarah was Ariel's friend. And Ariel was Sarah's *last* friend. Ariel had sworn that she would never let that bond die.

Anyway, breaking the code was probably easy.

Okay, that was pushing it. But it might be easier than it seemed. *Somebody* was meant to figure it out, right? What was that old saying? *The simplest solution is probably the right one.* The problem was that both she and Sarah had been intimidated. Sarah had always talked about how bad she was at math and solving puzzles. As if. But she had psyched herself out. And Ariel wouldn't let that happen. No way. Because what Ariel Collins lacked in humility, she more than made up for in confidence.

You can do it.

Of course she could. Damn right. She glanced over the outline again.

"Don't you want to go outside?" Caleb asked.

"In a minute," she muttered.

From what she could tell, Sarah believed that the code was either hidden in her English translations or in the original Hebrew, in this letter sequence stuff. And there was this part about the "primer" . . . a sort of built-in code breaker. The existence of a primer would make sense. *All* of it made sense, really—at least if Ariel understood it correctly.

So what if it was *all* true?

Maybe Sarah's mistake had been to assume that there was only one answer. Maybe the trick was to combine all of these theories into one. Ariel could look for a hidden message by skipping letters in the nonsense passages—but by using the *English* words because Sarah had translated them herself. In a way, it was the only choice Ariel had. She couldn't exactly teach herself to read Hebrew, even if Jezebel hadn't destroyed the actual scroll.

Caleb cleared his throat. "What are you *doing?*" he demanded.

"I'm not sure yet," Ariel mumbled. She sat down and dug a pen out of her pocket, then turned back to the prophecies. As quickly as she could, she copied down the nonsense on the facing page, removing all the punctuation and breaks between words.

toughcaremendsplawstrytokillnondefens irespellsslipsaffectsins

There. So now she needed to look at the first letter and skip . . . what? How many? Maybe four. In the original scroll there were nonsense passages under every *fourth* block of text. That could be a subtle way of letting somebody know that the number four was important: *Take one, count to four, do it again. . . .* Right? In fact, that could be what Sarah had meant by the primer: the built-in code breaker. It was worth checking out. Ariel wrote the long string again—only this time she capitalized the first letter . . . then the fourth . . . then the fourth letter after *that*. . . .

SougHcarEmenDszlQwstRytoKilMondEze nSiveSpelLsslSpsaFzecSsinS

A smile spread across her face.

There *was* a message. She hurriedly copied only the capitals:

SHEDARKNESSLSFSS

"That's it!" she shouted.

"Holy crap," Caleb whispered.

She started laughing—instantly, almost uncontrollably. An electric charge surged through her body. She was right! That was so freaking easy. It was right there. The primer *was* built right into the structure of the scroll. And the message was hidden both in Sarah's translation *and* the skip sequences.

"I did it!" she yelled.

Caleb's brow grew furrowed. "Are you *sure?*" he murmured.

"Take a look!" She jabbed a finger at the page. "'The darkness lifts. Eleven twenty-three ninety-nine.' What else could it be?"

"But—but you did it so *fast*," he stammered.

"I know." She shook her head, unable to believe it herself. "It just, like . . . *came* to me. I just saw it. All the pieces fell into place. Man." She slouched back in the couch, still grinning. "You know what? Now I can understand why Trevor got off so much on solving math problems. It's a *rush*. I'm serious. I know that sounds wack, but it's really intense. . . ."

She broke off.

Caleb was staring at the notebook. His face had become deathly white.

"What's wrong?" she asked.

"Ariel, don't you get it?" His voice quavered. "That prophecy came true. The darkness *did* lift today."

"Well, uh, yeah." Why was he being so dense?

"It came true, Ariel," Caleb cried. "That means this stuff *isn't* over. We were wrong."

My God.

Ariel's stomach lurched. Her eyes flashed back down to the page.

The False Prophet marches toward his own doom,
  Leading the blinded Visionaries to death with him.

If the prophecies were still coming true . . . if Leslie was still chasing the False Prophet, then there was a very good chance that *she* would be led to her death, too.

"What else does it say?" Caleb demanded.

But Ariel couldn't speak. There was also another bit of nonsense. Another coded message. Her eyes zeroed in on the bottom of the page, on the next date: 11/25/99.

Two days from today.

"There . . . there's something else," she whispered.

"What?" he cried.

She gripped the notebook. Her fingers had grown very moist. Trembling slightly, she wrote the first letter of the second message. . . .

God, no.

Her heart pounded. She kept writing and writing, letter by letter—

"Ariel?"

It can't be. Her hands were shaking violently now. Her chest tightened. *It can't be.* Using every remaining ounce of self-control, she forced herself to read the entire message out loud, in a voice that was barely a whisper. . . .

"Mount Rainier explodes."

Mount Rainier National Park
Washington
November 23-25

Harold Wurf was miserable.

He couldn't even enjoy the miraculous return of the sun. While his flock hooted and hollered all around him, he sat alone with Linda—rubbing his eyeballs and struggling to see something . . . *anything.* He'd made the idiotic mistake of staring up at the sky while the cloud broke and vanished, completely forgetting that his eyes might need time to adjust. It was so unlike him, so foolish. He only prayed his retinas weren't permanently damaged. Even after several hours he could still discern only fuzzy bits of light and glowing purple dots. He really wished he had brought some medical texts with him. Or at least an orthoscope.

"Don't worry," Linda soothed. She had to raise her voice in order to be heard over all the cacophony. "Your sight will return. It's only temporary."

Let's hope so, Harold thought with a scowl. He didn't understand it. He was the *Healer.* So why couldn't he heal himself? Why couldn't he simply *wish* for restored vision—as he had wished for Linda's restored beauty? It wasn't fair.

"The Chosen One has the power to cure others," Linda stated, as if answering his unspoken questions. "And on the appointed day you will have the power to transform yourself. I know it, Harold. Just as I knew the darkness would lift this very morning. You have to be patient. It will happen soon."

Harold snorted. It wouldn't happen soon enough. He was sick of being patient. He knew that the key to his powers lay in unselfish acts—but this was a little more extreme than he'd expected. Was it selfish to want to see again? That would seem to be the implication. For the first time in a very long while, he felt utterly powerless. Even more infuriating was that George Porter's obnoxious words kept running through his mind: *"You're a chump, Harold, and you don't even know it."* Well, maybe Harold was learning. Maybe now he *did* know. Only a chump would have made the mistake he did.

"I wonder what happened to him," Harold mumbled out loud.

"Who?" Linda asked.

"George Porter. I told you I saw him, didn't I?"

Linda patted his shoulder. "You didn't see George, Harold. You saw the Demon *disguised* as George. Remember what I told you? The Demon is very clever. She can take any form at any time. I left your side for an instant—and the Demon made one last futile attempt to sow the seeds of doubt inside you."

Harold shrugged. That sounded pretty goddamned far-fetched.

Then again, which was harder to believe—that the Demon had appeared before him or that George's

86

death was a hoax? *Neither* seemed very likely. It was probably best not to worry about it. Even if George was alive, he would be dead in less than forty-eight hours.

For that matter, so would the Demon.

Harold's eyesight worsened.

The glowing purple dots seemed to spread and cover his entire retinas. He could tell the difference between light and shade . . . but that was it. He couldn't walk without Linda's help. He was *crippled.* Here he was, the Chosen One—an exalted being—and he was stumbling around as if drunk and blindfolded.

"We have to get to the western slope," Linda kept saying as she dragged him up and down the uneven trails. "You have to get there by tomorrow."

Now he knew what it was to be a dog on a leash.

"Hurry!" she yelled.

Rage simmered inside his veins, but his only choice was to follow her lead. If he didn't, he would be helpless. Again and again he tripped and scraped his knees, tumbling into the dirt. Was this some kind of final test? Maybe he had to share the experience of the lowliest members of his flock in order to develop some kind of empathy. Maybe—

"You've really got to pick up your pace," Linda growled.

By the following morning his eyes had failed him completely. He couldn't see.

And he was no longer merely angry; he was *scared.*

He didn't know where he was—only that he had awakened to the sound of hundreds of voices and Linda's was not among them. Where on earth had she gone? Why had she chosen to leave him now of all times? He had no idea how to address his flock; he didn't even know what was supposed to *happen*. He'd been waiting for her to have another vision, another glimpse of the future in which everything became clear . . . but it never came. She *had* to be close by.

"Linda?" he yelled. "Linda, can you please—"

"Chosen One!"

Harold held his breath.

A girl was right next to him. She had a familiar Texas drawl. He knew that voice. But he hadn't heard it in a long time.

"It's me," the girl murmured. "It's Larissa."

Larissa. He sighed. He'd never imagined he'd be so relieved to run into *her* again. Yes. The lovely and dim-witted Larissa. He forced a smile, blinking at the nothingness. He could just picture those legs, that blond hair, that vacant smile. If it weren't for her, he might have never realized his true calling or ability. Not only was she the very first person he'd healed; she was also the only heretic he'd spared. Of course, her betrayal had been committed out of jealousy and love—not disrespect. She'd always believed in his powers. Not that such motives excused her. He'd sworn he'd kill her sooner or later. Thank God he hadn't. *Yet.*

"Are you all right?" she whispered. *Are yew ahll rah-ight?* She took his hand in her own. "What's the matter?"

He laughed shortly. "I can't see. Isn't it obvious?"

"I—I'm sorry," she stammered. "I didn't . . . What happened?"

"Never mind," he grumbled. "Have you seen Linda Altman?"

"The English girl?" There was a pause. "Yeah, but . . ."

"But *what?*"

She took a deep breath. "She's long gone. I saw her runnin' back up the other side of the mountain, like she saw a ghost or somethin'. I thought she mighta made you angry."

His lips twisted in a grimace. That couldn't be right. "Are you sure it was *her?*" he demanded. "Linda Altman?"

"Yeah, I'm sure. The one who's practically glued to your side, right? I heard her screamin' at people in that funny accent, yellin' at them to get out of her way. She looked scared. Well, scared or mad. But I'm sure it was her."

Jeez. Harold swallowed. Something was terribly wrong. He tugged at the ends of his long, greasy hair. Had she abandoned him? No . . . that was impossible. Had she had some kind of ominous vision? Had the Demon attacked her again? Maybe the—

"What is it, Chosen One?" Larissa murmured. "You don't look so good."

He didn't answer. A sickening thought was dawning on him. Linda had warned him that the Demon could only strike if he was alone. That the Demon was crafty. That the Demon could disguise herself as anyone. *Anyone.* Like George Porter, for example.

89

Or Larissa.

"Talk to me," she whispered.

My God . . .

She stroked his fingers. "I want to help you—"

"Let go!" he snapped.

In a fit of sudden terror he snatched his hand away—then fell flat on his back. He squirmed in the dirt. Rocks dug against his spine. His heart pounded. This wasn't Larissa. This was the Demon. It was the only plausible explanation for the insanity—

"I . . . I didn't mean anything," she whimpered. "Stop it! You're scaring me!"

What about me? The disguise was very deceptive. The silly Texas accent was utterly convincing. But he couldn't dwell on it. He needed to concentrate. The panic was insidious. If the Demon was here at his side, then Linda was most likely dead. Attacked again. Killed by the Demon while Harold was asleep . . .

The earth beneath him rumbled.

Magic, he realized. *The Demon's magic.*

"You can't do this," he muttered, whipping his head one way and then the other. "You can't defeat me. I'm the Chosen One. I'm—"

"What's happening?" Larissa's voice now came from far away. She sounded even more frightened than he did. "The mountain! The mountain . . ."

Her cries were lost in a sudden high-pitched wail. Hundreds of kids had started screaming. Harold blinked and blinked, praying in desperate horror that his destined moment would arrive this *instant*, that he would be healed and that he could stop whatever

cruel torture the Demon was wreaking upon his pre-
cious flock. That wasn't selfish, was it? No, no, no.
He wasn't thinking of his own needs. He *wasn't*. He
was here to help—

The rumbling grew more powerful.

Earthquake. Yes. He knew this sensation—the
feeling of being tossed about on the ground like a
broken toy. He fought to turn over, to flatten himself
out on his stomach, to reduce the risk of spinal cord
injury . . . but all at once he felt something heavy
land on his leg. On his back. His arms.

Feet, he realized. People's feet. Running.
Stampeding—over *him.*

His flock was walking on him, scrambling over
him. Crushing him. Bones cracked. Excruciating pain
shot through every limb. Harold fought to take a
breath.

"The volcano's blowing!" somebody shrieked.

Harold opened his mouth to scream but couldn't.
All the air had been forced from his lungs. Why was
his flock doing this? Why were they trampling him?
If Mount Rainier was erupting, then *he* could stop it.
Only he had the power. Only the Chosen One could
stretch forth his hand—

The agony abruptly ceased. He was numb.

Nerve damage, he realized with a blurry detach-
ment. It was as if his entire body had been injected
with an anesthetic. He was aware that people contin-
ued to run over his body and crush him, but his con-
sciousness was fading. And there was an odd,
whirring noise in his ears: a rapid *whoosh-whoosh-
whoosh.* . . . It kept growing louder.

It was right above him now. Hot wind blasted his face.

"Good-bye, Harold!"

Linda? Her voice sliced through the pandemonium. But it was tinny and distorted, as if it were coming from a loudspeaker. He couldn't tell where she was. . . .

"I'd take you with me, but there's no room in the helicopter," she called. "Lilith thanks you for all your help. We've got to be going. Cheers!"

The whirring faded.

Harold's mind swam. *No room in the helicopter.* Why had she said . . . "Lilith"? No. That couldn't have been Linda. Impossible. Because that would mean—*what*, exactly? He couldn't figure it out. His prized brain cells had been rendered useless. All he could seem to do was conjure up an image of George Porter's dirty little face: *"She's playing you, man. You and your whole freaking flock."*

And the next moment the image was gone.

In its place came a wondrous, liquid heat. It burned every thought clear from Harold's mind. There was no more pain. Just peace. He could hear a strange bubbling sound, as if a stew were boiling right beside him. It swelled in volume, louder and louder, closer and closer. . . .

Today I defeat the Demon, he thought dreamily. *Today I heal the flock—*

The heat rushed over him and consumed him completely.

CHAPTER
Novem TEEN

Babylon,
Washington
November 25

Oh, my God. I think Leslie's dead.

I sat outside all day, staring in the direction of Mount Rainier, praying so hard that nothing would happen, praying that the prophecies really were finished, praying that when the darkness lifted two days ago, it was just a coincidence. . . .

But then I saw it. It didn't even look real. A fireball lit up part of the southern sky. It was so slow. It looked like little meteors were flying out from it, shooting in all directions, like fireworks in slow motion.

The weirdest part was, I didn't hear a thing for a really long time. Just the wind blowing and the birds chirping. Like watching TV with the sound off. Then the ground began to shake a little and there was a noise, like the lowest note on a bass guitar played through an amplifier cranked on ten.

And then it was over. That was it. A thousand kids might have died. Ten thousand.

Maybe Leslie wasn't with them. I have to hold on to the hope that she made it out of there in time. I have to. I can't take it, losing her, too. How many people have I lost now? Sarah. Trevor. Brian. Jezebel, even. And Dad.

Please don't let Leslie be dead.

Caleb couldn't stand to watch. He's inside, crying. And I know it isn't just because of Leslie, either. It's because he's scared for us. Terrified. So am I.

Because this means that Sarah didn't

stop anything. She didn't put an end to the countdown.

She died for nothing.

Now I know why I still have that awful feeling inside. The prophecies are still coming true. The explosion proves it. Whatever terrible thing is supposed to happen at the end of the twelfth lunar cycle is still going to happen.

But how can that be? Except for the stuff in the codes, almost all the prophecies are about the Demon and the Chosen One. So are Jezebel and Sarah still alive somehow?

That's the only way it makes sense. Maybe their spirits are still here. Maybe they don't need bodies. I don't know. How can I? I just want a sign, something that will answer these questions for me. Is that too much to ask?

Sarah . . . if your spirit really is

still out there, will you let me know? Will you tell me why nothing has changed, why everybody in this town just marched off to their own deaths without even knowing it, falling right into the Demon's trap?

I wish I'd never figured out that stupid code. Then I wouldn't know any of this. Then I would think that everything was fine.

I should have gone with you, Leslie. I'm so sorry.

PARTmber

November 26-30

The Eleventh Lunar Cycle

"Flesh she will eat, and blood she will drink!" cried the Lilum, dancing in wanton abandon around the sacred fire. Their black robes flapped like wings. "Flesh she will eat, and blood she will drink. . . ."

Naamah's eyes filled with tears.

The joy she felt was beyond description. She had fulfilled Lilith's grand plan, disposing of the Seers in an eleven-month-long campaign—an odyssey that started in Arctic Russia and brought her halfway around the world to the Pacific Northwest . . . a hundred miles from the site of the Final Battle.

Looking back on all the Lilum had achieved, she was filled with wonder and pride—but most of all with a sense of completion, of wholeness. Her work was done.

A job that had begun three thousand years ago was over.

Long ago the ancient prophets had foretold that the earth itself would cry out in terror when Lilith arose again. The terror would manifest itself in a series of disasters: earthquakes, floods, avalanches—as well as plagues of locusts and darkness.

All of it had come to pass. And more.

Yet the Scribes had desperately wanted to keep this knowledge hidden from their enemies. Their hope was that these natural forces would work against Lilith . . . perhaps even destroy her. And so they had encoded the exact dates and locations of every calamity in their magic parchment for use three thousand years hence, when the Chosen One appeared. Indeed, their code was designed in such a way that only someone born at the end of the Second Millennium could possibly find it. Or so they thought.

Little did they know that the Lilum had used their own black arts to copy the scroll and break the code long ago, passing the wisdom down from generation to generation . . . waiting for the moment when they could transform the words into weapons.

Thanks to the Scribes, the Lilum knew to attack the Russian base in Poulostrov Kanin precisely when the solar flare wiped out its power . . . to blast the

Aswan High Dam precisely when the Red Sea flooded . . . to trap a group of Seers in the Rockies precisely when the avalanche struck . . . while the Chosen One herself wallowed in ignorance.

The intricate strategy had produced a thousand stunning victories on an unimaginably grand scale. But the Lilum were not content to use only the knowledge hidden in the codes. They took the battle a step further, employing technology when the earth's self-destruction was not enough, luring the Seers into various traps with false broadcasts. . . .

But the manipulation of the final two hidden prophecies was the greatest accomplishment. It was a double blow, a perfect combination. First the Seers were led astray, then they were annihilated. Their pull had drawn them toward Babylon— and when the darkness had ruined their powers, the Lilum took over, diverting them to Mount Rainier.

When the cloud lifted, their sight was restored.

And they believed that Harold was responsible. So they heeded the call to join him on the western slope. They waited for his blessing, even as they wondered why they still felt the pull to some other place, why they felt certain that the Chosen One was a girl. . . .

Poor Harold. Naamah smiled. A true champion of Lilith. Her only regret was that he had blinded himself. She'd wanted him to bear witness to his own destruction—to see her waving from the helicopter, to see the lava rushing over him and all the thousands of believers who had called him "Healer."

But she could live with the disappointment.

Because in the end, every single Visionary but two had been killed.

The Blessed Ones still remained at large. Naamah now knew who they were. Then again, she supposed she'd always known. But it didn't matter.

George Porter and Julia Morrison would soon be dead as well. She didn't have to concern herself with them. Lilith would handle those two herself.

And in one week's time Naamah would gaze upon her master face-to-face. She would feel Lilith's embrace—an embrace given substance by magic and prophecy. She would witness the detonation of the ancient weapon, when all the unworthy would perish . . . when only those whom Lilith had chosen would inherit the earth.

Sweetest of all, she would stand at Lilith's side to rule the new world.

**Babylon,
Washington
November 26**

Babylon was empty.

George couldn't believe it. Nobody was here. He'd spent the last two days wandering from one end of town to the other—up to that weird engineering college, down to the mall, back to the cliff—and he hadn't seen a soul. Where the hell was Sarah? And everybody else? This place had been *packed* when he'd split. Packed. There had to be some kind of explanation. An entire *town* didn't just get up and disappear. Unless . . .

His eyes wandered down Puget Drive—toward the southeast.

A huge, fluffy ash-gray cloud hung in the blue sky there, rising up from the suburban homes and evergreens . . . frozen in space like a giant clay model. He swallowed. It looked so close. *Too* close. And how far was Mount Rainier? A hundred miles?

Still, he wasn't sure if it was coming from Mount Rainier. He was jumping to conclusions. He'd been walking around yesterday, minding his own business, when he'd heard this strange rumbling noise. And

105

okay, it had come from that general direction. Then he'd looked up and seen . . .

It doesn't matter. Sarah wouldn't have gone there.

Nah. No way. Maybe she'd met up with Julia and some of the other Visionaries and taken them to some special place that he couldn't find. Maybe they were hiding from the Demon, figuring out a way to destroy her. That sounded right. He shoved his hands in his grubby black pockets and marched determinedly up to a little rise in the road. Sure. He would find them. *Today.* It was just a matter of time.

A strange queasiness shot through his gut.

He paused. He *knew* this spot. This was near where the Demon lived. He and Sarah had been tearing up this hill—and they'd nearly run over a bunch of kids, all waiting to flush Ariel out of her house. Then that freak Jezebel stabbed Ariel and Ariel just plucked the knife out of her chest like nothing had happened—

Smack!

"Ow," he muttered.

He absently rubbed the side of his neck. The unseen hand was slapping him again. Good. He needed a smack every now and then. Otherwise he'd get lost in his own thoughts and start freaking himself out. How many times had the hand hit him in the last three days? Fifty, maybe? As soon as that cloud had broken and the sun started shining—*boom.* He was a Visionary again. Just like that. Hell of a ride. He couldn't go more than two hours without passing out and seeing all the old familiar sights: the baby, that spot on the cliff—

Smack!

He shook his head and started walking. In a weird way, he was kind of glad all the Visionary stuff had come back. Even the pain. At least he knew he was in the right place again. And if *he* felt it, then Julia would feel it, too. She wouldn't have gone to Mount Rainier. Of course not. She knew the truth. . . .

"Hey!" a voice called.

George jerked. He froze in his tracks. He *wasn't* all alone.

Some skinny guy with scraggly brown hair was standing on a lawn, about five houses down, waving both hands at him.

"Hey!" the guy called. "Isn't your name George?"

Hold up. George knew this dude. His name was . . . what? Colin? Something like that. He was friends with the Demon's brother—that guy Trevor. They'd been up at WIT, trying to find a cure for the plague. Or so they said. There was something sketchy about them.

"Ariel!" the guy yelled. "Come here!"

George gasped. *Ariel?* The queasiness he'd felt before turned to full-fledged nausea. He recognized that house, too: two stories, white wood . . . it was the Demon's. He was—

The door flew open.

Ariel strolled out and squinted at him. Then she frowned at the guy.

"What's going on?" she asked.

This isn't happening. She looked exactly the same as he remembered—only without the knife. He'd seen enough. He whirled around and sprinted back down the road.

"Wait up!" the guy called. "I just want to . . ."

But George didn't slow down. His feet pounded on the pavement. His lungs tightened. *Gotta hide.* He'd bolted from the cops dozens of times in Pittsburgh when a second's delay would have meant arrest. But those escapes were leisurely strolls compared to the way he was running now. He kept his eyes fixed on the line of gray water beyond the trees in front of him. He supposed he could dive into the ocean . . . but no, it was a long drop. He'd kill himself.

Without thinking, he turned to the left when he hit the fork at the end of the road.

His thighs were starting to burn. *Move!* he commanded himself. He could hear the waves crashing at the base of the cliff on the other side of the trees. The smell of salt water filled his nostrils. He was coming up to that spot . . . the spot he had seen in his visions. *Bad idea.* The Demon would probably look for him there first. But it was almost as if he couldn't help it. Even in terror he was drawn . . .

Uh-oh.

Dizziness swept over him.

He stumbled slightly, throwing his hands out to balance himself. He suddenly found he could hardly breathe. He felt as if he were on a merry-go-round. What the hell was his problem? Was he out of shape?

Tightening his jaw, he forced himself to keep running. But his legs were getting stuck in quicksand. *No, no.* That couldn't be right. He was having trouble seeing. His stringy blond hair flapped in his face; sweat stung his eyes. The twisting highway swirled in a blur. The sun faded. He blinked once, then again. . . .

When I stand on the cliff and look out at the ocean under the clear night sky, I can't believe that I'm in any kind of danger. A cool breeze blows. The reflection of the moon dances in the water. It's all so tranquil.

But I am afraid.

My baby is crying. Tears fall from her eyes, and she screams—but there's nothing I can do. I squeeze her as tightly as I can. I can hear the Demon laughing all around me. I turn to look, but all I see are tall hourglasses . . . a whole forest of them, and every single one is empty.

And then my baby is gone. I hold nothing in my arms . . . nothing at all.

The Demon laughs. "Time's up!" she cries. "The baby is mine!"

George opened his eyes.

He found he was staring up at a sky full of stars. He took a deep breath and sat up straight. Was this still part of his vision? No . . . he was definitely awake. His breathing was even. He wasn't sweaty. He actually felt pretty well rested—

Holy crap.

He was on the cliff! There was the ocean, right in front of him. He sat in the gravel by the side of the road. He staggered to his feet and spun around, half expecting to see a bunch of oversized hourglasses, or

Ariel, or maybe some girls in black robes . . . but all he saw were those tall pine trees, swaying gently in the wind.

Chill, he told himself. He crouched down in a boxer's stance and turned a full three-hundred-sixty degrees—fists raised, eyes and ears alert. The night was very quiet, except for how long it was . . . a few hours? A few days? He shuddered. It seriously creeped him out. He'd been totally unconscious. Anything could have happened to him in that time. *Anything.*

He glanced back at the road.

Instinctively he began walking toward it—in the opposite direction of Puget Drive. Ariel's house was only a five- or ten-minute walk from here. Why hadn't she chased him? She and her helpers had spent the entire year trying to hunt him down . . . him and all the other Visionaries. Why stop now? Was she toying with him? Was it some kind of game? He wouldn't be surprised. That chick Amanda and all her Demon-worshiping friends had toyed with him for weeks before they tried to kill him.

Just to be safe, he glanced over his shoulder— then hesitated. *Hmmm.* No sign of Ariel, but something else caught his eye: a little mound of stones by the woods on the other side of the road. Strange. He hadn't noticed that before. Of course, he was always looking the other way, out toward the ocean.

It almost looked like a monument.

Actually, it looked like the kind of weird prop Amanda and her buddies would use—like those stone circles he'd seen in Ohio and Mount Rainier.

He scurried across the pavement and bent beside the pile, squinting at it in the pale light of the moon. Somebody had sloppily painted a few words on its base. . . .

Here lies the body of Sarah Levy

The Chosen One

May her memory live forever

What the hell?

He drew in his breath, reading the words again. His pulse quickened. This had to be some kind of prank. The Demon was screwing with his mind.

No way Sarah was dead. No way—

All the warmth seemed to drain from his body, leaving only a frigid emptiness. He stumbled away from the stones. He felt as if he were going to puke.

This *was* a real grave, wasn't it?

Yeah. Even as he fought to deny it, he knew it was real. Why else would Sarah be missing? Why else would the town be empty—except for the Demon and that guy? Ariel had probably killed Sarah and chased all the rest of the Visionaries out. Or maybe Ariel had killed the Visionaries, too. Maybe she'd tricked them into going to Mount Rainier, along with everyone else. Maybe he was the only one left to eliminate . . .

Oh, God.

An even more terrifying thought crept into George's brain.

What if he wasn't worth the trouble of killing anymore?

Of course. That was why Ariel hadn't bothered coming after him. It didn't matter whether he lived or died. He was probably the only Visionary left. He *had* to be. No wonder he couldn't find Julia. She was dead, just like the rest of them. And without her—without the others, without the Chosen One—he couldn't do a damn thing.

The sand in the hourglass was gone.

"Time's up." The Demon had said it herself. Everybody who could stop her had been killed. Including Julia.

CHAPTER TWELVE

187 Puget Drive,
Babylon, Washington
Early morning, November 27

"So who was that guy again?"

Caleb paced around Ariel's living room, wringing his sweaty hands. "I *told* you," he muttered. "George somebody—I can't remember his last name. A friend of Sarah's. A Visionary. A *powerful* Visionary . . ."

But Ariel just slumped back in the couch. There were dark, puffy circles under her eyes. How could she be so tired? She'd slept all day. The only time she'd even left the house was to take a quick peek at George. Then she'd gone straight back to bed. Maybe she should try to scrounge up some coffee. Or some stimulants. This was *important.*

"Ariel!"

"Wha?" she slurred. She blinked a few times. "What's wrong? I know who he is, all right? I remember now. Sarah talked about him. She said he drove her across the country, then ran off to find his girlfriend. So what's the big deal?"

"The big deal is that he ran off to Mount Rainier!" Caleb cried.

She didn't answer. It didn't even look as if she'd *heard* him. She simply gazed back at him with that

113

same glazed, heavy-lidded expression—as if she'd gone on a major drug binge.

"Ariel, what's the matter with you?" he yelled. "Don't you understand what this means? If George went to Mount Rainier and made it back, then he *survived*. And if he survived, then maybe other people did, too. Like Leslie."

That seemed to get her attention. She jerked up, eyes widening. "God," she whispered. Her hoarse voice cracked. "Maybe you're right. Why didn't you tell me earlier?"

He flashed a strained smile. "Because you've been up in your room all day, like some kind of . . . kind of . . ." He was too flustered to finish.

"What?" she demanded.

She was sitting very straight now. Her jaw was tight.

"I don't know," Caleb muttered, turning away.

He was going to say *mental patient*. Which was true. Ever since Mount Rainier had blown up, she'd slipped into this weird, zombielike state. Totally catatonic. Meanwhile Caleb had been driving himself crazy—unable to sleep, unable to *eat* (or even drink)—wondering if Leslie and everyone else in town had survived, wondering if he and Ariel should have chased after them, wondering why Ariel didn't seem to give a crap anymore. . . .

"Excuse me if I haven't been myself," Ariel snapped in the silence. "I'm a little depressed, you know? It's kind of hard to keep smiling if everybody you've ever known or cared about is *dead.*"

Caleb blinked.

Dead. He felt as if she had literally *punctured* him with that word. He'd sprung a leak . . . and all the anger was flowing out. He stared at her. She was right. Their friends were gone. Every one.

"I'm still here," he whispered.

Ariel's eyes filled with tears. "I know," she croaked. "I don't want to argue with you, Caleb. It's just . . . I'm scared, okay? I don't know what's going to happen to us."

He sat beside her and wrapped his arm around her shoulders. "But that's what I've been trying to tell you. We *can* figure out what's going to happen to us. You cracked the code. We've got the prophecies. I mean, if we knew before what was going to happen at Mount Rainier, we wouldn't have let . . ." He shook his head, unable to complete the thought.

"I just can't look at that notebook anymore," she sobbed, falling against him. "I'm sorry. It hurts too much. I'm so sorry—"

"Shhh," he soothed. He patted her on the back—as if that would actually *help*. She was really losing it, wasn't she? He'd never seen her like this. No matter how bad things had gotten in the past, she'd always held it together. *He* was usually the one who freaked out first. Maybe he should just put her back to bed. He could take a look at the notebook himself. If he could find it. Ariel's room was a hellhole. He might have better luck trying to track down George. Yeah. He could deal with some fresh air, actually. . . .

Ariel sniffed. "What's wrong?"

"Uh . . . nothing," he mumbled. "I was just wondering if I should go look for George."

"I doubt you'll find him. He's probably long gone by now."

Caleb's brow grew furrowed. "Why? I mean, he must have come back to Babylon for a reason, right? Aren't the Visionaries *pulled* here or something?"

Ariel shrugged. "Maybe. But it didn't really look like he wanted to hang out, did it?" She nestled against his chest and closed her eyes.

No, it didn't. Caleb leaned back, staring absently into space. Something had seriously spooked George. The look on his face . . . it was one of *terror.* But what could have done it? He'd been standing there, staring at Caleb. If only he knew. If only he knew what *Caleb* had gone through to prove Jezebel was lying . . .

Blecch.

Memories of those drunken nights with Jezebel began to drift up from the recesses of Caleb's brain. He cringed slightly, shifting in his seat. Still . . . it could have been worse. Much worse. A lot of times he actually *forgot* who he was dealing with. Jezebel was really pretty pathetic in a lot of ways. She was insecure and petty, for one thing. And aside from being able to read minds, she couldn't do much else. She tried to act tough and scary and self-assured—but looking back on it, she was sort of weak. Caleb had been scared a lot of times, but the fear came more from the *idea* of what was inside Jezebel . . . not the girl herself.

Now, Ariel . . . *she* could be a lot more threatening.

He glanced down at her. Her eyes were shut; her chest was slowly rising and falling in sleep. He shook his head. She looked so peaceful.

Maybe he'd been a little hard on her these last few days. She *had* suffered. Not just recently—but in the past, too. There was all that stuff with her mom, for one thing. Not to mention the fact that Jezebel had plunged a knife right into her heart . . .

His smile faded.

Hold on a minute.

How *did* Ariel survive that?

It didn't make any sense. Ariel had supposedly survived that attack because of Jezebel's magic. So Jezebel had the power to save Ariel's life, but she couldn't save her *own?* But maybe the Demon didn't need a human body anymore. That was what Ariel had said when the mountain blew up. The Demon was still alive. The Demon *had* to be alive. The prophecies were still going.

But other things didn't seem to fit, either. Now that he thought about it, Jezebel's powers were also blamed for making all those Visionaries melt whenever they came near Ariel. So Jezebel could *kill* people with magic—but for some reason, she needed a gun to kill Sarah.

Why?

He shivered once.

A very unpleasant theory was forming in his mind.

What if people were wrong about Ariel? What if she *was* the Demon after all?

What if it was the other way around? Maybe Ariel had set Jezebel up by using her *own* powers. That would have been clever. Very clever. In spite of the fact that Jezebel was a lunatic, she had always insisted that she *wasn't* the Demon. Nobody believed her, of course—but who would be a better scapegoat? Ariel could have used Jezebel to kill Sarah . . . which would mean that the Chosen One was dead, but the Demon wasn't. Maybe *that* was why the prophecies were still coming true. If one of them was alive, that was enough.

And Caleb knew that Ariel was a skilled liar: manipulative and sneaky. She'd *bragged* about it. She'd also cracked the code—very easily, and conveniently *after* all the Visionaries had gone off to be blown to bits. Not even the Chosen One could crack the code, but Ariel could. Ariel, who had the only copy of the translation.

In the end, Ariel had gotten *everything:* the notebook, the secret prophecies . . . all of it.

And she was the only one left standing.

So there was a chance that George knew something that Caleb didn't. There was a chance that George *did* recognize Ariel. A big chance.

Caleb stopped breathing. It wasn't just a theory anymore. No. It was very, very real.

He jumped up from the couch and ran to the door.

"Hey," Ariel mumbled sleepily. "Where are you going?"

But he didn't answer. He simply closed the door behind him and took off into the dawn.

THIRTEEN

**Babylon,
Washington
Afternoon of November 27**

I can't believe it—I actually made it
here. After all those months of feeling
that pull to go west, I'm finally here.
Now the pull is like a magnet, pointing
straight at the ground. I'm centered.
I'm home. I could almost be happy if I
weren't so lonely and afraid.

Those kids were right. Babylon is
deserted.

Still, it's where I need to be. Thank
God, Bob and Ted agreed to keep driving
me here. It was either that or leave
me on the side of the road. I guess I
got a little hysterical. I couldn't help it.
The pain I felt when that black cloud
broke . . . I'll never forget it. It was

like every single vision I've had in the past year had been trapped by the cloud and now they were all coming at once. I was glad, though. Because the return of my visions and of the pull showed me that the battle isn't over. I still had to come west. To come here.

I have to fulfill my visions—and my destiny, whatever that may be.

Bob and Ted are good people. I was wrong to doubt them. They wanted to stay with me until I had the baby, but it wasn't their problem. They brought me to Babylon, and that's enough. I could tell they were relieved when I told them to go.

The Demon is very near. I can feel it.

But I'm not as scared as I thought I would be.

I actually feel hopeful. Because I saw my baby for the first time. In a vision. She's so gorgeous. She has one brown eye and one green . . . one of

George's and one of mine. And I know that the other Seers were right. She is special.

She inherited that strength from her father. And she inherited second sight from both of us. Now that the Chosen One is dead, I know that my daughter must be the only hope

Julia took a deep breath and wiped her forehead. It was pretty hot for the end of November. Maybe she should get out of the sun. Sitting here probably wasn't the best thing for her already weakened condition. The cool shade of the nearby pine trees would offer relief. But she couldn't seem to stray from this *one* spot, even only a few feet. . . .

I wish you could have made it, George, she thought, closing her diary. *It's just as beautiful as you said it would be.*

Her lips curled in a melancholy smile. Even if the pull hadn't drawn her to this cliff, she would have found it, anyway. George's description had formed an image in her mind long ago: the way the frothy waves broke on the rocks below, the way the blue-green ocean stretched out toward the hazy horizon. . . . It was exactly right. Her gaze wandered down the green coast to the southwest, following the broad curve of the highway, all the way down to a snowy mountaintop far in the distance.

Which mountain *was* that, anyway?

Well, she knew it wasn't Mount Rainier.

A shiver shot up her spine. A few days ago she'd been gazing at Mount Rainier from the highway when it started spewing vile black smoke, shot through with what looked like lightning bolts. A few minutes later, glowing red lava dripped from the top. It looked so *close*—even though it was probably forty miles away. Then the whole top of the mountain just blew apart. Bright bits of fire cut through the sky, leaving trails of smoke behind them. After several long seconds the ground started shaking. A low thunder filled the air. Little white specks rained down on the highway. Gradually all the smoke blocked what remained of the mountain from sight.

Nobody had said a word, though. There was nothing to say. Bob and Ted never mentioned it once. And Julia guessed that she could understand their reasons.

They had friends on that mountain.

So did she, for that matter. Harold's entire flock had been there. She didn't want to think about it. So many kids had been fooled. So many lives had been wasted. . . .

Maybe the question wasn't: *What mountain am I looking at?*

Maybe the better question was: *Will that mountain explode, too?*

She slowly pushed herself out of the gravel and stood. *Whoa.* Her head swam for a moment. She really *should* get out of the sun. Her protruding belly was like an anchor, weighing her down. She almost felt the way she did before she slipped into a vision . . . dizzy, queasy, disoriented—

Good Lord.

Somebody was creeping up the road, sticking close to the woods, crouching down as if trying to hide. Julia frowned—she hadn't even heard anything. She held her hand over her eyes to block the sun and squinted down the road. It was a guy. Short and skinny . . . with long blond hair. He was wearing dirty black jeans and a black T-shirt.

Julia froze.

A sick feeling filled the pit of her stomach. He was maybe forty feet away, but he looked a lot like . . .

Their gazes met.

He stopped in his tracks.

The hairs on the back of Julia's neck stood on end. Her heart rattled violently in her ribs. This couldn't be happening. Of course not. That boy was the mirror image of . . . even from here she could see that he had bright green eyes—

His eyes widened.

"Julia?" he called.

Her knees instantly turned to jelly. *The voice, too.* He came shuffling toward her, his black Dr. Martens kicking up dust.

"Julia?" A trembling smile spread across his face. He broke into a jog. "Julia?"

I must be dead. I must be—

The next instant he was squeezing her in an embrace. She blinked several times, staring over his shoulder at nothing. He was *crying*. Sobbing

123

uncontrollably. His body shuddered in her arms. He ran his fingers through her matted hair.

"I was gonna leave," he wept. "I tried, but I couldn't. It hurt too much. And I tried not to think about you, but I couldn't help it." He sniffed. "Tell me you're here. Tell me this is real."

She opened her mouth.

But her lips and tongue were dry as leather, incapable of forming words.

"Am I . . . am I dead?" she finally choked out.

George stepped away from her. His dirty face was soaked with tears . . . but it was more beautiful than she had even remembered it—like a painting of Cupid or some other impish Roman god. His cheeks were flushed. His eyes glimmered in the afternoon sun.

"Of course not," he whispered.

She swallowed. "But *you're* dead."

He shook his head. "No."

Her throat tightened. "Is this a vision?" The words were almost lost in the wind.

"No, no!" He laughed and wiped his eyes. "Julia, I'm *alive!* I didn't die at Harold's farm. I *escaped.* I got out. I fooled them all. Even you."

She shook her head. Her eyes grew blurry. With a quivering hand she reached up and touched her own cheek. *She* was crying, too. She hadn't even noticed. This couldn't be real. Miracles didn't happen. Not to her. Never to her . . .

"Julia." His gaze drifted down to her belly. "Are you . . ."

"It's yours," she whispered.

He glanced up. His face suddenly came alive with that wild, inner light—that magic look of understanding that she'd noticed from the start . . . and she knew then that she *wasn't* dead or unconscious. She was awake and living. Because that expression could never be forged, even in a dream. It was what had drawn her to him. It was what had sealed their love.

"It's not mine," he said. "It's *ours.*"

FOURTEEN

187 Puget Drive,
Babylon, Washington
Night of November 28

It took Ariel an entire day to figure out exactly *why* Caleb had ditched her.

Or maybe she knew the answer all along. Maybe she was just too horrified to accept it. But she kept running down a list of arguments in her mind—and none of them fit except one.

Caleb thinks I'm the Demon.

The scariest part of all was that she couldn't blame him.

Nope. It sure as hell *looked* as if she were the Demon, right? Here she was, alive and well—and all her friends (and enemies) were dead. Pretty amazing. Why had she even bothered trying to fight it? For months and months the answer was clear. Visionaries dropped dead around her. Her former best friend, Jezebel, went psycho on her—but *ha!* The joke was on Jez. Ariel was immortal. So once again it all came back to the same question Ariel had asked herself every single day until she had met the Chosen One: *If I'm the Demon, then how come I don't know it?*

That seemed like a reasonable thing to ask.

She sat up in her rumpled, unmade bed. The candles in

127

her room had almost burned out. The Mickey Mouse clock ticked away on her bureau: *ticktock . . . ticktock. . . .*

It was almost midnight. The funny thing was, she'd been lying here amidst the clothes and garbage and filth for hours now, knowing that there was probably an easy solution to this dilemma—but simply being too terrified to act on it.

Well . . . maybe it wasn't so funny.

Her gaze fell to the coffee-stained red notebook on the carpet. Sarah's notebook. The translation of the ancient scroll.

The answers were in there. All she had to do was open to page one and start reading. Then she would know for sure. Then she could find Caleb and reassure him and prove him wrong.

Or right.

She swallowed. Just looking at the notebook filled her with dread. Her pulse was already rising. She hadn't been able to open it in five days—not since she'd broken the code. She didn't *want* to know what else was predicted in there. She might learn something about herself that she didn't really want to know.

But you have to do it.

It was true. Not knowing was worse than knowing. The torture would never end if she didn't figure this out once and for all. Besides, Caleb had a right to know, too. For that matter, so did everyone else in the world. Like that guy George What's-his-face. She had to . . .

Go on!

She grabbed the notebook off the floor and flipped open to a random page. She'd start anywhere. Why not? If the prophecies fit, they fit.

The Demon will wreak havoc upon the lands and seas . . .
And the servants of the Demon will bring death wherever they tread.

All right. This was the third lunar cycle. March. What had she been doing in March? Not wreaking havoc upon the lands and seas, at least as far as she knew. No, if memory served her correctly, she'd been sitting around the Citicorp Building in Seattle, getting wasted. She sure as hell didn't have any *servants,* either. Sarah used to call the Demon's servants the "girls in black robes." Well, they hadn't done a damn thing for Ariel. She'd never even *seen* any of them. She glanced down at the next portion.

To be heavenly raises us.
Deals make it safer for all fools to read lips.
Three twenty-seven ninety-nine.

Code, obviously. Ariel fumbled around for a pen. By the dim light of the candles she carefully copied down every fourth letter under the date.

THEREDSEAFLOODS

Wonderful. If she was the Demon, she'd flooded the Red Sea on March 27. Now how in God's name could she have done *that?* She didn't even know where the Red Sea *was.* Wasn't it in the Middle East or something? She couldn't help but laugh. She was a pretty good Demon, wasn't she? She didn't even have to know geography.

Shaking her head, she turned the page to the next lunar cycle. The month of April. This wasn't so bad, actually. In a totally twisted way, it was even kind of enjoyable. There was some stuff about the sun and the Seers. . . . *Bor-ing.* She skimmed down to the part about the Demon.

. . . While the Demon assumes a human form,

Walking among the righteous and the wicked.

Seen but not seen. Heard but not heard,

Her name will be sealed within a name,

As the dark secrets are sealed within this scroll.

Ariel nodded to herself. Sarah had talked a lot about this part; it helped prove that *Jezebel* was the Demon. Not Ariel. April was the month when Jezebel had lost her marbles. *Something* had happened to her—namely, the old Jezebel disappeared and the Demon had possessed her, "taking a human form."

The prophecy fit. Plain and simple.

So what had happened to Ariel during that time?

A lot, actually. That weird Visionary gave her the

necklace. She also nearly *died* when the Sheraton burned to the ground. But Leslie saved her life. . . . Still, she hadn't assumed any form other than her own. She was the same old jerk she'd always been.

Wasn't that enough? Did she really need to keep doing this?

No. She *wasn't* the Demon.

She was starting to get angry, and she wasn't even sure why. Maybe it was because these stupid prophecies were reminding her of some things she regretted—like how she'd wasted that entire month being a bitch to Leslie, when they should have been friends from the start. And now Ariel would never have a chance to make it up to her. . . .

Don't think like that. You don't know for a fact that Leslie's dead.

She glanced back down at the notebook: *"Her name will be sealed within a name, as the dark secrets are sealed within this scroll."*

Sealed within this scroll. The code, obviously. But did that mean the Demon's name was a code, too? Hidden in code like the prophecies were hidden in the nonsense passages?

Ariel felt the color drain from her face.

The letters hidden in Jezebel's name didn't spell anything. She knew that instantly.

J . . . B . . . O . . . nothing.

What about my *name?* she thought, almost afraid of the answer.

ARIELCOLLINS

With a trembling hand she decoded it.

Arie̲LcolL̲ins

ALL. Now what was that supposed to mean?

Frantically Ariel began writing down names—everyone she'd ever known. Sarah Levy—*SHY*. Ariel smiled a tiny bit. Sarah *was* shy, but that didn't seem worthy of some ancient code. Shouldn't it have said *Chosen One?* Maybe she'd misunderstood. Maybe there was no code like this.

Caleb Walker—some nonsense word. Trevor Collins—nonsense. Leslie Tisch—nonsense.

Ariel smiled for real this time. If Leslie could see her now, she'd roll her eyes and laugh at Ariel—*Ariel!*—sitting here trying to decode some prehistoric mystical thing.

God, I miss her, Ariel realized with a pang. She knew in her heart Leslie was gone, but if she closed her eyes, she could practically feel her best friend in the room with her. *Maybe I should decode her entire name,* Ariel thought. Leslie had always loved all her stupid middle names.

LESLIEARLISSIRMATISCH

She quickly began to solve the code. Reading the names she knew so well—first with a faint spark of humor, then with growing panic . . . and finally with horror.

L̲esl̲I̲ear̲L̲issI̲rmaT̲iscH̲

𝓛 ↲ 𝓛 ↲ 𝓢 H

COUNTDOWN
to the
MILLENNIUM
Sweepstakes

$2,000 for the year 2000

5...4...3...2...1 MILLENNIUM MADNESS.
The clock is ticking ... enter now to
win the prize of the millennium!

1 GRAND PRIZE:
$2,000 for the year 2000!

2 SECOND PRIZES: $500

3 THIRD PRIZES: balloons, noisemakers,
and other party items (retail value $50)

Official Rules
COUNTDOWN
Consumer Sweepstakes

1. No purchase necessary. Enter by mailing the completed Official Entry Form or print out the official entry form from www.SimonSays.com/countdown or write your name, telephone number, address, and the name of the sweepstakes on a 3" x 5" card and mail it to: Simon & Schuster Children's Publishing Division, Marketing Department, Countdown Sweepstakes, 1230 Avenue of the Americas, New York, New York 10020. One entry per person. Sweepstakes begins November 9, 1998. Entries must be received by December 31, 1999. Not responsible for postage due, late, lost, stolen, damaged, incomplete, not delivered, mutilated, illegible, or misdirected entries, or for typographical errors in the entry form or rules. Entries are void if they are in whole or in part illegible, incomplete, or damaged. Enter as often as you wish, but each entry must be mailed separately.

2. All entries become the property of Simon & Schuster and will not be returned.

3. Winners will be selected at random from all eligible entries received in a drawing to be held on or about January 15, 2000. Winner will be notified by mail. Odds of winning depend on the number of eligible entries received.

4. One Grand Prize: $2,000 U.S. Two Second Prizes: $500 U.S. Three Third Prizes: balloons, noise makers, and other party items (approximate retail value $50 U.S.).

5. Sweepstakes is open to legal residents of U.S. and Canada (excluding Quebec). Winner must be 20 years old or younger as of December 31, 1999. Employees and immediate family

members of employees of Simon & Schuster, its parent, subsidiaries, divisions, and related companies and their respective agencies and agents are ineligible. Prizes will be awarded to the winner's parent or legal guardian if under 18.

6. One prize per person or household. Prizes are not transferable and may not be substituted except by sponsors, in event of prize unavailability, in which case a prize of equal or greater value will be awarded. All prizes will be awarded.

7. All expenses on receipt and use of prize, including federal, state, and local taxes, are the sole responsibility of the winners. Winners may be required to execute and return an Affidavit of Eligibility and Release and all other legal documents that the sweepstakes sponsor may require within 15 days of attempted notification or an alternate winner will be selected.

8. By accepting a prize, a winner grants to Simon & Schuster the right to use his/her name and likeness for any advertising, promotional, trade, or any other purpose without further compensation or permission, except where prohibited by law.

9. If the winner is a Canadian resident, then he/she will be required to answer a time-limited arithmetical skill-testing question administered by mail.

10. Simon & Schuster shall have no liability for any injury, loss, or damage of any kind, arising out of participation in this sweepstakes or the acceptance or use of a prize.

11. The winner's first name and home state or province will be posted on www.SimonSaysKids.com or the names of the winners may be obtained by sending a separate, stamped, self-addressed envelope to: Winner's List "Countdown Sweepstakes", Simon & Schuster Children's Marketing Department, 1230 Avenue of the Americas, New York, NY 10020.

Printed in the United States
By Bookmasters